BOY OF BLOOD

Girl of Glass, Book Two

MEGAN O'RUSSELL

Ink Worlds Press

Visit our website at www.MeganORussell.com

Boy of Blood

Cover Art by X Potion Designs (https://www.x-potion.net/)

Editing by Christopher Russell

Interior Design by Christopher Russell

Printed in the United States of America

DEDICATION

For Jessica

BOY OF BLOOD

CHAPTER ONE

Drops of bright red streaming and swirling into nothingness. Deep red from someone.

Someone's veins had been split open. Were they dead or still clinging to life?

The blood didn't care as it was washed away. Swept down the drain by the pure water of the domes.

Nola's sobs echoed off the shower walls, blocking out the sounds of the outside world. She knelt on the floor, watching the blood turn from crimson to pink as the burning water removed all traces of the battle. Someone knelt beside her, washing her, murmuring comforting things she couldn't hear. They combed their fingers through her tangled curls, removing bits of glass and dirt.

She should look. See who was taking care of her. But what did it matter? As soon as they knew what she had done, they would disappear. Or she would. They would learn the truth. Then Nola Kent would vanish.

Strong arms wrapped her in a towel and carried her to her bed. Outside the window she caught a glimpse of the rain pounding down on the dome. But the storm wouldn't taint Bright Dome.

Nola's home hadn't been harmed. They had destroyed her world but left her home. A poor attempt at pity.

Something sharp pierced her arm.

"Hush," Jeremy whispered. "It'll help you sleep."

Before Nola could say she didn't deserve sleep, darkness took her.

Her mouth tasted of cotton and blood when she woke. Her arms and legs were heavy, like someone had buried her alive. But they hadn't. She lay in her bed as though nothing had happened. A beautiful orchid sat on her desk. Jeremy had brought it for her.

A flower for his girl.

It might have been a century ago.

Nola bit the inside of her mouth, willing herself not to scream. Footsteps on the stairs finally made her sit up in bed. Someone had dressed her in her mother's robe. It smelled like Lenora Kent. Fresh flowers, earth, and strong cleaner.

She rubbed her hands over her face. Her fingers found the bandage on her neck as her bedroom door swung open.

Jeremy walked in, balancing a tray of food. A smile lit his tired face when he saw Nola.

"You're awake." Jeremy set the tray down and sat next to her on the bed. "I wasn't sure you would be yet."

"You gave me something to sleep?"

"The doctor did." Jeremy brushed a dark brown curl from her cheek.

"Doctor?" Nola thought back, trying to find where in the blood and tears a doctor had come near her. "I don't remember a doctor being here."

"Two days ago," Jeremy said. "He put the patch on your neck, too. He said you should be okay now. No permanent damage."

She kicked free of the covers and stood, tipping sideways and knocking into her desk.

Jeremy grabbed her around the waist before she could take another step toward the mirror. "Careful."

"I want to see it." Her fingers trembled as she pulled off the pale-pink patch on her neck. Two thin, white marks showed on her skin. Shaped like teardrops and barely raised at all, they were the only trace that a Vamper had bitten her, tried to kill her only two days ago.

"The doctor can work on it some more," Jeremy said, his deep brown eyes meeting Nola's in the mirror. "He'll get rid of the scars."

Nola studied her reflection. The dark curls belonged to her, but the face had changed. Paler and harder. She looked more like someone from the outside than a girl who'd spent her life in the safety of the domes.

"I don't want him to fix the scars." Nola turned away from her reflection and didn't fight as Jeremy drew her into his chest. He was so tall, and his well-muscled shoulders so broad, it felt as though he could fold her into his body and protect her from the sun itself.

Safety is just another myth.

"It happened," Nola said. "The domes were attacked, I got bit, and people died. We can't make it not true, and I don't want to pretend we can."

"Okay." Jeremy kissed the top of her head. "If that's what you want, we'll make the doctor leave the marks alone."

She stood in Jeremy's arms, waiting for something to happen. For a siren to sound or fire to rip through the Kents' tiny house. But no crashing danger came. No screams, no flames. Just Jeremy. His smell of fresh earth that matched the domes mixed with the starch in his new guard's uniform. Jeremy, warm and steady, holding her up even when she couldn't find the strength to hold him.

"What's happened?" Nola asked, when the silence grew too loud to bear. "Since...since I fell asleep."

"Not much." Jeremy guided her back to the bed. "The rain stopped for an hour that first night, and we scrambled to get the places where the domes were shattered fitted with temporary covers. But that's about all. The wounded are all out of the medical wing and back home except for the worst few. And the dead—"

"They can't be burned until the rain stops." Nola's empty stomach churned at the thought of the line of dome dead waiting their turn.

"With this much acid rain, we haven't been able to go into the city to see if any of the Vamper scum who did this to us are still there, but on the plus side—"

"They'll be stuck wherever they are, too." She tried not to picture Kieran hiding underground with the others from Nightland, packed into dark holes, desperate not to get burned. But Kieran had betrayed her, had betrayed the domes. He had led the Vampers into her home and stolen from the domes. Innocent people died because of him.

Because I trusted him.

Her hands shook, and her breath came in ragged gasps.

"Nola, we're safe here." Jeremy kissed her palm. "No one is going to get back in here to hurt you. I won't let them."

"Jeremy," Nola said, fighting to keep her voice steady enough for her words to be understood. The time had come to tell the truth, to rip open the terrible wounds before they had more time to heal. "When I was with the Vampers from Nightland—"

"Jeremy," a voice called from downstairs. "Is Sleeping Beauty still out?"

Jeremy smiled at the sound of his sister's voice. "Nope, but you would've just woken her up anyway."

Footsteps sped up the stairs, and Gentry Ridgeway stepped into Nola's bedroom. Her eyes lingered on the robe Nola wore for a moment before she spoke. "All people able to move and not on guard duty are to report to the Aquaponics Dome in twenty minutes. There's a meeting about the plan for moving forward with..." Gentry gestured to the walls around her as though to say *our existence.*

"I'll be there soon," Jeremy said.

"Nope." Gentry shook her head. Her dark blonde hair she wore barely longer than Jeremy's ruffled around her face, making her, for a moment at least, appear softer than the fierce Outer Guard she was. "You *and* Nola will come now." Gentry held up a hand when Jeremy began to argue. "She's awake and can move, she has to come to the meeting."

"It's fine," Nola cut Jeremy off when he opened his mouth to argue again. "I'm fine. I'll come to the meeting."

"Good," Gentry said. "We need everyone who's left to work their asses off to get this place put back together. Every single one of us will have to give our all for the domes to survive." Gentry said the last words to her brother, giving him a hard look before walking out of the room.

Nola waited for the sound of the kitchen door closing before looking back to Jeremy. "Does Gentry not think you're doing your part? I mean, you're not even eighteen yet, and you're already an Outer Guard. Why would she—"

"That's not what she said." Jeremy took her hand, carefully helping Nola to her feet. "And that's not what she thinks. We lost a lot of people and a lot of supplies. The domes have to be repaired, and now there are a bunch of rogue Vampers who've declared an all-out war on us. The domes were built to help us survive in this broken world, and now the world is trying to break us. But there is no way in hell I'm going to let them." Jeremy leaned down, brushing his lips against Nola's. "I promise."

It took Nola longer than normal to pull on clothes. Every muscle ached as she dragged her shirt over her head. Her fingers burned as she tied the laces on her work boots. She didn't have the will to force her curls into a tight braid, so she let her hair hang wildly around her shoulders. Just another thing knocked out of place in the strict order that preserved the domes.

She let Jeremy lead her down the stone paths that cut through the grass and wildflowers, weaving past the willow trees and tall maples that made up the green spaces of Bright Dome. Even the roofs of the houses had been planted with thick moss. Every detail had been planned to make the most of the precious space within the glass.

Dome perfect.

But not anymore. Bright Dome had changed since she stumbled through it after the attack. Sleeping bags and boxes of food hid beneath the dangling tendrils of the largest willows. Neat piles of clothes nestled next to the bubbling fountain.

"Some glass in Low Dome and Canal Dome got cracked." Jeremy followed Nola's gaze. "The rain isn't getting in, but the Council doesn't want people sleeping in there. We moved most of the singles into the Guard barracks, but the families had to find other places."

"So, they're sleeping on the ground?" A knot formed in Nola's throat. "They're sleeping in the dirt like the homeless in the city."

"Not like in the city." Jeremy led her away from the makeshift camp, down the stairs and into the tunnels that were the paths between domes. "In the city, the people who sleep outside aren't safe. Here, they are. They're fed and guarded, and it's only for a few days. As soon as the rain stops, we can get Low Dome and Canal Dome fixed, and everyone can go home."

She nodded, not trusting herself to speak.

The cleaning crews had been busy in the tunnels. There was no glass from shattered lights left to crunch beneath their feet. All traces of blood had been scrubbed from the floor. The normality of it, the cleanness, was worse than the blood had been. Horrible things had happened. Mopping the floor wouldn't make it go away. It would have been easier to see the horror. To point to it and scream *this is why I am broken!* But the halls were scoured to perfection.

People packed the Aquaponics Dome by the time Nola and Jeremy arrived. Half-buried with the fish tanks sitting below ground-level, the dome was dark at the best of times. With the storm raging outside, it was impossible to tell if it was night or day down by the meeting, where the department heads stood in a line in front of the fish.

Hundreds of people crowded together. Some in work uniforms, others in normal clothes. The sight of them all jammed together like animals set Nola's nerves on edge. But worse was the fact that they all fit. There should have been more of them. Enough people to spill up onto the stairs. There should have been chatter and laughter bouncing off the glass. But the only sound was the dull hum of the fish tank pumps. The people stood silently as if the funerals had already begun.

"People of the domes," Captain Ridgeway, Jeremy's father and the head of the Outer Guard, addressed the crowd, "we have come upon a dark and terrible time. Our mission has always been, will always be, to protect the people, plants, and animals that are in these domes. We do not do this for our own survival but for the survival of the human race. To protect our children's children. Since the domes were founded, those who live on the outside have coveted the resources we hold, right down to the clean air we breathe. But never before has a group maliciously tried to destroy mankind's best chance for survival." Captain Ridgeway paused, surveying the crowd. "They tried to destroy us, but what they don't understand is that we learn. We have learned where we were weak, we have learned the depths to which they will sink to annihilate us, and we will never allow them the opportunity to attack the domes or its people again."

The crowd clapped and cheered. Shouts of "For the domes!" and "Destroy the Vampers!" carried over the din.

Captain Ridgeway held up a hand, and the moment of celebration faded. "We have a lot of hard work ahead of us. Sacrifices must be made to push forward for a better, stronger future than the domes have ever dreamed of before. Together we will stand strong. Together we will push forward. Together we will become the future the world needs us to be!"

The shouts of the crowd echoed off the glass, drowning out the sound of the thunder beyond.

CHAPTER TWO

"I just want to help," Nola said for the hundredth time as she followed her mother through the seed cold-storage room.

"Magnolia, I don't have time for this," Lenora snapped, moving to the next row to check the temperature of the seed trays.

"You would have more time if you let me help you!" Nola let her voice ring off the walls.

Lenora stopped moving and pinched the bridge of her nose. "I know you want to help. You are a wonderful girl who wants to help the domes, and I appreciate that more than you will ever know. But right now, the most important thing is to protect these seeds. Without these seeds, the people in the domes could starve, and even if we managed to survive on corn, we would leave nothing for future generations to bring back out into the world. The Vamper scum stole three boxes of my seeds, and now with the dome repair, I can't trust the air system to be reliable. I'm sorry, Nola, but the most helpful thing you can do is leave me to my work."

Nola stood for a moment, teetering on the verge of shouting again. "Right. Sorry, Mom."

She turned without giving her mother a chance to say another word and stalked past the shelves upon shelves of seeds, not stopping until the cold-storage door *whooshed* closed behind her. Nola leaned against the concrete wall of the hall, letting the panic of being three stories underground take her. Her vision swam and her heart raced. Every nerve in her body told her she would be crushed to death at any moment. The panic at being so far below the surface was better than the terrible fear and self-loathing that filled her aboveground, surrounded by the blatant signs of attack.

The seeds were stored deep under the earth in the safest place the domes had to offer, but still the attackers from Nightland had gotten into seed storage and medical storage right next door. More than thirty feet of hard-packed earth above and the Vampers had gotten in and out. They had known where they were going and exactly how to get past the guards. Nola's hands shook. She dug her nails into her arms, willing herself not to scream.

Footsteps came toward the door of medical storage. Nola pushed away from the wall and hurried down the hall, past the guards, and up the stairs.

"Miss Kent," the sharp voice sounded as soon as she reached the landing on the next level.

She froze for a moment before dashing up the next flight of stairs.

"Miss Kent, I need to speak with you immediately."

Nola turned slowly, not needing to see his face to know Captain Stokes was the one calling her, his black eyebrows pinched at the center as he glared at her.

Captain Stokes was the head of the Dome Guard, the ones who protected the domes themselves. Just as Captain Ridgeway was the head of the Outer Guard, the elite unit that patrolled the streets of the city across the river, fighting on the front lines when riots overtook the decaying slums.

It was Captain Stokes' men who should have stopped the

attack from ever happening. His Guard who had failed five days ago.

"How are you, Captain Stokes?" Nola's voice wavered as the powerfully built man approached her.

He limped, still favoring his right leg after the battle, but that didn't make him any less intimidating.

"My fallen guards are up next for burning, the ones who are still alive are protecting the shattered side of the domes, and the damned doctors can't set my leg properly," Stokes said. "How well do you think I'm doing, Miss Kent?"

"About as well as the rest of us," Nola said. "Everyone's lost something, Captain Stokes."

"But was everyone surprised by the loss?" Stokes narrowed his eyes. "I need to talk to you about your time as a prisoner in Nightland."

Though she had been expecting his words, her heart began to race.

"You told us you had only seen the inside of your cell when you first came home, but when the attack came, you became a fount of information." Stokes leaned closer, backing her into the wall.

The knowledge that Captain Stokes had every right to glare at her like he knew each horrible thing she had done didn't make it any easier to not run away.

"How to navigate the tunnels of Nightland, how to find their leader's home, even where they had been storing things aboveground. I'd like for you to explain to me how you knew all those things if you never left your cell, Miss Kent." Stokes' face was only inches from hers, but something in the foul stench of his stale breath emboldened her.

"What happened to me in Nightland was outside the domes," Nola said. "What happens outside the domes is Captain Ridgeway's concern, not yours. If Captain Ridgeway wants to talk to me, he knows where to find me. In the meantime, why don't you go check on your guards? Make sure no more of them end up in line for burning."

She sidestepped Stokes and darted up the stairs, not breathing until she had reached the lights of the dome two stories above. Sunlight touched her face as she gasped for air. Even through the glass of the dome the sun warmed her skin.

Her feet carried her toward Amber Dome, away from the workers with their heavy boots and noisy tools that toiled frantically to fix the side of the atrium before the rains returned. Back down a flight of stairs and into a short tunnel. Heavy panes of glass leaned against the wall, waiting to be used in the atrium. But the steel had to be fixed first. It would take days for the wall to be in place, and no one knew how long for decontamination to be complete.

The steps leading up into the Amber Dome were empty, and the few people tending the crops in the low, wide dome didn't pay Nola any mind. The vents blew in clean air, and the fans lifted the scent of fresh, moist earth and vibrant leaves. Rows of leafy green vegetables ran along the outer edge of the dome, closest to the glass, but she headed straight for the center, to the middle of the wheat field that swayed in the breeze. She ducked her head low as she walked so no one could see her path, and when all the walls were out of sight, she lay down on the warm soil, letting the green and amber stalks surround her.

Thick, gray smoke cut through the dazzling blue sky above. Ten would be burned today. Ten of the seventy-two fallen Domers. A list had been read over the com that morning. PAM had displayed their faces on all the computer screens for ten minutes, one last memorial to those who had died. This was the third day of burning, and they hadn't even made it to the fallen guards yet. They would be burned last, their sacrifice in protecting the domes given the highest point of honor.

Twenty-seven guards had been lost.

Nola rolled onto her side, covering her head with her arms.

Twenty-seven guards who wouldn't be there to defend the domes if Nightland attacked again.

But the Vampers from Nightland had fled the city. Taken everything they had and vanished. They could be hundreds of miles away by now. Or only a few. Kieran had never told her where it was Emanuel, the leader of Nightland, wanted to take his people.

She took a shuddering breath. Pain shot through her, but there were no tears. How could she cry for herself when she knew what was to come?

She had thought before that Nightland would never attack the domes. She had been delusional enough to believe she knew Emanuel and Kieran. That they were good people who would never harm her or her home.

Seventy-two dead.

Her home had been shattered. She had to pay the price, but she would be damned if she was going to wait for Stokes to come for her. Nola looked back up to the bright sky. The smoke had started to fade. Another body gone. Scrunching her eyes, she tried to memorize the bright blue. She might never see the noon sky again. But the blue held no thrall. No lightness or joy. All that was left for her was justice and darkness. She stood and, walking tall, headed straight for the Iron Dome.

CHAPTER THREE

Two Dome Guard flanked the steps to the Iron Dome. Neither of them attempted to stop Nola from passing. Neither of them called her a traitor or tried to haul her away. It would have been simpler if they had. It would have spared her from having to tell the world herself.

I don't deserve for this to be easy.

The Iron Dome was wide-set with low bushes instead of trees to ensure sightlines in case of attack. It was the only dome where metal could be lowered to shield the glass from destruction and the only dome where weapons were allowed. But Nightland had attacked the exact opposite side of the complex, leaving the Iron Dome completely untouched.

Nola approached the largest of the shoebox-shaped houses. A shadow moved past the kitchen window as she climbed the steps to the Ridgeways' door.

Good. Better to get it over with. You've made up your mind. Now do it.

Her hand didn't shake when she knocked. Almost instantly the door swung open, and Jeremy stood in front of her.

"Nola." He beamed down at her as though finding her at his door was the most wonderful thing he could imagine. "Come on in." He took her hand and led her into the kitchen, pulling her into his arms as soon as the door closed.

His heart pounding quickly in his chest couldn't compare to the speed at which Nola's raced.

"What are you doing here?" Nola stepped the foot away from him the tiny kitchen allowed. "You're supposed to be on duty."

"I got switched to night patrol for today, so I got sent home to rest," Jeremy said. "But you must have—"

"I need to talk to your dad," Nola said. "I need to see him right away."

"So, you didn't come to say hi to me?" Jeremy gave her a joking smile.

She couldn't find it in herself to smile back. This wasn't how it was supposed to go. She was going to tell Captain Ridgeway, and have it done. All at once. No more complications.

"Where's your dad?" Nola asked.

"He's not here." Jeremy stepped forward, taking her face in his hands. "He's out in the city. There was some trouble, and he wanted to check it out himself before tonight."

"Dammit." Nola scrunched her eyes shut. She needed to do it now, but there was no way they would let her go out into the city to find Captain Ridgeway.

"Nola," Jeremy said, wrapping his arms around her, "you're okay."

"Don't!" She shoved Jeremy away and started for the door, but Jeremy was faster. He stepped in front of her, blocking her way out before she could even reach for the handle.

"Nola, what's—"

"Get out of my way, Jeremy."

"Nola, what do you—"

"I said get out of my way!"

Jeremy flinched as though she had hit him. Strong Outer Guard Jeremy, who fought Vampers without fear, flinched because she had yelled at him.

"Please," she whispered, dragging her fingers through her tangled hair, relishing the pain it caused. "Let me go."

"No," Jeremy said. "Not until you tell me what's going on. Nola, I love you. I know you're hurting and scared. After what you've been through in the last few weeks, anyone would be. So I can't just let you leave if you're this upset. I love you, and I'm scared for you. It's my job to protect you."

"Please don't say that." Her words barely squeezed through the tightness of her throat.

"But it's true. I love you, and whatever you need to talk to my dad about, whatever has got you so upset, I'll do whatever it takes to help you." Jeremy stepped forward, wrapped his arms around her and kissed her. "I love you, Nola Kent."

"Please don't." Tears trickled down her face.

"I can't help it." Jeremy brushed away her tears. "I love you."

Nola looked into Jeremy's brown eyes. He loved her. He truly did.

Her heart shattered, like a physical blow to her chest, bending her in half with the pain of it.

She sank to the ground, willing herself to stay present, to not slip away into the terrible agony of it all. The hard way would be better for Jeremy. Breaking him now would allow him to heal.

"Nola, are you all right?" Jeremy's eyes went wide with fear. "I'll call a doctor."

"I'm a traitor." The words rushed from her as though they had been waiting for their chance for weeks. "I betrayed the domes, and everyone that died is dead because of me."

Jeremy's brow wrinkled, but she didn't stop. He needed to know everything. She had been selfish in wanting to tell Captain Ridgeway. It was Jeremy her betrayal would hurt most. He deserved to hear the horrible truth first.

"I didn't mean to. It didn't start that way," Nola pushed on. "It started at the Charity Center the day of the riot. Kieran Wynne was there. He stole my I-Vent. He told me if I needed him, I could find him at Nightland."

Jeremy turned away, but Nola grabbed his face, forcing him to look at her, making sure he heard every awful word.

"I wasn't going to go after him, but then someone with dome medicine was killed on the streets. I needed to know if it was him. I broke out and went into the city. I knew the way through the glass—one loose pane. One stupid, loose pane I had known about for years. Kieran was alive, but I met Emanuel, the leader of Nightland, and his little girl. She was dying. A little girl was dying, and they needed more medicine. I stole it for them. I thought I was done. I thought she was saved and it was over, but then you said the guards were going to raid Nightland, and Kieran, Emanuel, and his daughter would all have been killed. So I left through the glass again to warn them. I was never kidnapped. I went to warn them."

"They stabbed you, Nola." Jeremy latched onto the one thing that could prove her innocence.

"They thought I was a guard. I stole a coat to stay safe in the rain. They thought a guard was attacking. They didn't mean to hurt me. But by the time I woke up, it was two days later. Emanuel said the kidnapping story was the only way to get me home. I didn't even know if I wanted to come home, they all seemed so good. Trying to feed the city, trying to build a new world for everyone, but Emanuel said it was the only way to prevent a war, and they had to send me back. I trusted him. I trusted Kieran."

Nola spoke through her sobs, feeling Jeremy's anger growing, but it wasn't over. Not yet.

"They taught me a lie. What to tell you had happened. That they had taken me and locked me up. But they didn't tell me how horrible living with the lie would be. Being here in the sunlight and knowing how many good people were trapped in the dark. I wanted to go help them. That's why I wanted to leave. I would have gone. But then they attacked. I didn't know they were coming. I swear to you I didn't.

"I never thought they would attack my home. But they did. Kieran was here with the others. I saw him. He was stealing from the domes while the Nightlanders were murdering our people. I didn't know, I promise I didn't know that they were going to attack. But it doesn't matter. I betrayed the domes. I betrayed you and my mother, and everything the domes are supposed to stand for."

She took a breath, her body hollow now that the flood of words had left her. Hands trembling, she let go of Jeremy's face, wiping away her tears before speaking again. "I have to tell your dad. I'm a traitor, and I have to face the consequences. I am so sorry, Jeremy."

He looked away at the sound of his name. She couldn't blame him for never wanting to see her again.

"I did terrible things, but I never ever wanted to hurt you," Nola whispered as she pushed herself to her feet. "I'll go wait in your dad's office till he comes back. Please don't tell anyone till I talk to him. I just want to get it done."

"Don't," Jeremy said, pressing his palm to the door so she couldn't open it. "Don't you dare walk out of this house, Nola."

She froze as Jeremy sprang to his feet, not taking his hand from the door.

"I have to go," Nola said, her voice barely above a whisper. "I have to tell—"

"Don't you dare tell me what you have to do." Jeremy took Nola by the shoulders, pinning her against the counter. Fury flashed in his eyes.

She didn't blame him. She couldn't. She was a murderer standing in his home.

"Your father will turn me in to the Council." An eerie calm filled Nola. "They'll decide what to do with me."

"No, they won't, because you aren't going to tell any of them a damned thing." Jeremy's face was inches from hers, but she didn't look away. "We lost seventy-two people in the attack on the domes and six when we tried to rescue you."

"I'm sorr—"

"Don't!" Jeremy shook her. "Seventy-eight people are dead. Don't you dare tell me you're sorry! The domes lost more than a tenth of our people. A tenth of our carefully-calculated population designed to save the world. And now you want to strike out one more? Because you feel guilty?"

"I have to tell them! Stokes knows I lied. He knows I saw the tunnels in Nightland!"

"Stokes is a moron! Stokes is one stupid man, and you're just going to have to keep lying to him, because we are already losing too much! Look at this." He dragged her to the window, making her look out at the fresh waves of dark smoke blooming in the sky. "There is too much grieving and too much loss here, Nola. You don't get to add to it. We need you, and if that means you have to live with the guilt of hiding what you've done, so be it."

"You don't need me," she said, grasping for the words that would make him understand. "You would all be better off without me."

"You're being trained in plant preservation." Jeremy spun her to face him. "We need you to keep feeding our people."

"There are other people who can do that job."

"And what about when your mom cracks up? She can't lose you, Nola." He gripped her shoulders. "I can't lose you. I won't."

"People are dead because of me." A fresh wave of tears tumbled down her cheeks at the look of horrible desperation in Jeremy's eyes. "I am no good to anyone. Least of all you!"

"Did you ever want to betray the domes?" He shook her. "Did

you ever for one minute do something that you thought would hurt us?"

"No. I thought I was helping. I just helped the wrong people."

"I won't lose you because you made a mistake." He pulled her to his chest, his strong arms surrounding her like a steel vise. "There is too much at stake to lose you, too."

"But I have to pay for what I did." She leaned against Jeremy's chest, certain if he let go for an instant she would fall.

"Pay for it by helping the domes survive." His breath was ragged as he whispered. "Pay for it by making the world a better place."

"But Stokes wants to talk to me."

"Lie." He lifted her chin and stared straight into her eyes.

"I can't."

"You aren't allowed to say you can't. Promise me you'll lie."

"How can you even want me here? How can you even stand to look at me?" She laid her hand on his cheek, willing him not to slip away. For him not to be a part of a terrible dream.

"Because I love you," he said. "I love you because you are good and kind and want to help everyone. Those Vamper scum, they lied to you. They manipulated you. Whether you see it or not, they hurt you and used you. But I won't let their abuse take you away from me. I fought too hard to get you back."

"I don't deserve for you to love me." Nola pressed her lips to his cheek. "I'll never deserve it."

Jeremy turned his head, his lips brushing gently against hers. She pulled herself to him, wrapping her arms around him, willing herself to believe that this was real. He was there, holding her, protecting her. After all the blood and pain, he still believed she was worth saving.

Nola's heart raced as his fingers found the skin at her side, tracing a line toward her ribs. She deepened their kiss, stumbling when he pulled away.

He took her hands in his, staring at them for a moment before kissing both her palms.

"Promise me one thing," Jeremy said, still looking at her hands. "Promise me you aren't still in love with Kieran Wynne."

She took his face in her hands, staring deep into his brown eyes. "If I ever see Kieran Wynne again, I'll kill him myself."

CHAPTER FOUR

*R*eport *to the Amber Dome at 0800 for planting. You have been assigned a supervisory role. Report to Lenora Kent for further information.*

The message started blinking on Nola's bedroom wall at six in the morning. PAM woke her up, beeping as the words lit the darkness.

Magnolia Kent. You have received an assignment from the Dome Reconstruction Committee. Please tap your screen to confirm receipt.

Nola climbed out of bed and tapped the screen in her wall before PAM could continue. It was the first assignment she had received since the attack. Everyone else who wasn't in the hospital had been given a task but her. She had assumed the Council had deemed her too broken or too much of a liability. But there it was, blinking on her bedroom wall. The domes wanted her to work. Or at least her mother did. Dressing quickly, she popped her head out of her bedroom door, listening for the sounds of her mother. Silence filled the house. Lenora had been sleeping in her office for the last week, coming home only to shower.

Grabbing two apples from the counter, Nola started toward

the door. She could go down and see her mother and still make it back to the Amber Dome in time to work.

She froze with her hand on the doorknob. She'd been summoned to the Amber Dome. One of the domes that hadn't been damaged by the attack. Whose walls were still solid with no cracks to the outside world.

The air in there would be clean. It was safe to work on plant preservation. There was no chance of acid rain contaminating the workers. But there would be no chance of her trying to run either.

Mom doesn't know. Only Jeremy knows.

Nola exhaled, forcing her lungs to remember how breathing was supposed to work. She wouldn't let the panic that floated right under her skin take control, not when there were useful tasks to be done. She was alive and in the domes. She had a chance to be productive and people were counting on her. She had lost the luxuries of fear and self-loathing.

She opened the door and walked slowly out into the bright morning sun. The vents above pumped in fresh, cool air, their low humming a battle cry against the heat of the outside world.

This is part of my punishment. Living with the lie. I'll never be sure if someone knows what I've done.

She reached the bottom of the steps to the tunnels and instinctively headed, not toward her mother's lab or even the Amber Dome, toward Jeremy's house. He should be home from his night's work in the city. He was probably asleep. But he wouldn't mind Nola waking him.

Nola smiled to herself, her first real smile in weeks. Jeremy would be happy to see her even if she only had a minute.

She ran the rest of the way through the tunnels, waving at the Iron Dome guards as she passed. One of them smiled and waved back, not bothering to hide his chuckle. She stopped below Jeremy's window, her panting from running so long swallowing the laugh that bubbled in her chest.

She reveled in the foolish feeling of standing under his window in broad daylight.

"Jeremy," Nola called up softly. "Jeremy!"

The window opened a moment later, and his face appeared. Though his cheek was marked with lines from his pillows, his eyes were alert the moment he saw her.

"Nola, what's going on?" he asked.

"Nothing." She shrugged. "I just wanted to see you."

In one swift movement, Jeremy jumped out his window, landing silently in front of her.

Without a word, Nola wrapped her arms around his bare stomach, laying her head on his chest.

"Are you sure you're okay?" He held her close, pressing his lips to the top of her head.

"I'm—" She stopped herself before speaking the comforting lie. "I have a work assignment today, in the Amber Dome."

"That's good." He leaned back just enough to look Nola in the eye. "You'll be helping."

"I know, and I want to, I do. But everyone else is working in the atrium or in the Grasslands Dome where the real damage is. What if my mom knows? What if..." All the happiness Nola felt at seeing Jeremy faded away. Her hands shook at the thought of her mother knowing what she had done. Lenora wasn't like Jeremy. She wouldn't forgive the way he had.

"Shhh, you're okay." He took her trembling hands in his. "I talked to your mom."

"You what?"

"I told her she needed to stop treating you like you couldn't help," Jeremy said. "She'd been keeping the Council from giving you an assignment because she thought you needed more time to heal. I told her you would be better off helping."

"But not near the breaks in the glass?" Nola's throat tightened.

"You aren't medically cleared for it." Jeremy's brow wrinkled. "You were with the Vampers and in the open air too long. The

Council is worried about people getting contaminated with the outside air coming in, and you're at the top of the list of people who have been overexposed."

"But you and the other guards have been going out every day. If you can go into the city—"

"That's different. It's our job." He tucked Nola's hair behind her ear. "And they make sure we're okay. They take care of us."

"But why not do the same for me? I want to help, I don't want anything with Nightland to stop me from doing what I can—"

"They won't let you, Nola." He grimaced, resigning himself to something very unpleasant. "You're a girl."

"What?"

"You're a really smart girl, with really great DNA," he said quickly, as though ripping off a bandage. "The doctors are worried about birth defects in the next generation if the young women are exposed to the outside air. So, they're pushing all the women away from working on the breaks in the glass to *protect future generations.* It's not just you, I promise."

"Well," Nola began slowly, "at least it's not because they think I'm a liability or a traitor."

"There is that." Jeremy gave a tight smile.

She glanced at the house. "Does the ruling go for guards, too? Are they going to try and keep the female guards in the domes?"

"Yeah."

"And how does Gentry feel about that?"

"Not good." Jeremy wrapped his arms around Nola. "She's furious, and I can't blame her."

"Can she fight it?" She pressed her cheek into the warmth of his chest.

The Outer Guard were the elite. The ones who had chosen to risk their lives every day for the protection of the domes. Nola's father had been an Outer Guard and had died in service to the domes. If anyone had ever tried to keep him inside, they would have had one very angry, very skilled man on their hands.

"How can you fight what's for the good of the domes?" Jeremy said.

"You can't," Nola said. The weight of the truth hung heavy in the air. "So, I guess I should get to the Amber Dome. Where the young women go to work." She leaned up to kiss him.

Jeremy brushed his lips against hers. "Thank you for waking me up." He kissed Nola again. "I think you should do it more often."

"Me, too." She kissed him on the cheek and walked away, holding onto his hand until their fingers couldn't touch anymore.

CHAPTER FIVE

Six guards flanked the steps to the Amber Dome, all wearing full riot gear. Nola hesitated in front of them, unprepared to meet a full complement of guards in her brown gardening jumpsuit. But the first guard nodded at her to pass. She hurried up the steps, finishing the braid in her hair as she entered the vast space of the Amber Dome.

Lenora stood with three guards on a high platform in front of the patch of wheat. Nola's shoulders tensed at the sight of guards in the middle of the garden.

Amber Dome housed most of the domes' edible crops. Rows of vegetables bordered trellises that supported vines bearing heavy tomatoes and gourds. The placid greenery held no threat for the guards to defend against.

"Magnolia," Lenora called as Nola approached. "How are you?" Her mother looked her over from head to toe as though searching for a sign that even being asked to work was enough to make Nola crack.

"I'm good." Nola forced a bright smile. "I'm happy to have something productive to do."

"Good." Lenora reached down to help her daughter up onto

the waist-high platform. "And you won't just be working, you'll be supervising. We are going to have to move more plants in here. We lost animal feed from the grasslands, and we can't let the stock starve."

"Right," Nola answered, still trying to listen to her mother as movement at the stairs caught her eye.

"It's not desperately complicated, and with the men in the department working in the Grasslands Dome, the muscle trying to rebuild the walls, and everyone in the technical departments trying to purge toxins from the domes' systems, we've had to get a little creative with the workforce."

A dozen people emerged from the staircase. People Nola had never seen before, dressed in the worn clothes of city dwellers.

"I'll be up here supervising the operation, and you'll be down there making sure none of the outsiders damage our plants. They've all been cleared and seem competent, but I doubt they know much about agriculture."

Guards herded the outsiders toward the center of the dome. A look of something between amazement and fear showed on each of their faces.

"Mom, we aren't supposed to have outsiders in the domes," Nola said.

"Desperate times, Magnolia. The Incorporation couldn't send help from any of the other domes, so this is what we have to work with," Lenora said. "They build sets of domes all over the world to ensure future generations of children have a shot at living. They meddle in every decision we make from how much iron we get in our diets to what plants I should grow. But ask the Incorporation for some extra help after you've been attacked by thieving murderers, and this is their solution."

She turned to the outsiders who now stood at the foot of the platform. "Thank you all for joining us." Lenora spoke in a bright voice that sounded nothing like her usual tone. "You will be broken up into four groups for planting tasks. With any luck, we can get all of this done over the next few days. We genuinely appreciate your assistance during the domes' time of need."

Lenora ignored the stony looks the outsiders gave her as she issued instructions. Nola was one of four who had been chosen to supervise the outsiders. The other three Domers were also women, all under thirty. Jeremy had been right. They hadn't assigned her here out of fear she would run. They were trying to protect the women.

Disgust mingled with relief as Nola led her group of three workers to the lattice side of the dome. Past the tall stacks of pots where the leafy greens grew and the coated pipes with tiny sprigs of herbs peeping out the side, to where vines bound with thick twine wrapped around metal poles.

Trays waited at the end of the long line of vines. She didn't need to ask her mother what task they had been assigned. The tomatoes were ripe. They needed to be harvested and sent down to food collection. Then the vines that weren't useable anymore would be trimmed away, making room for newer plants to join the lattices. Nola had been doing the same job for years. Only the workers were new.

"Right," Nola said, trying to sound more confident than she felt as she turned to face the outsiders. "Thank you for coming to help us today." She realized how horrible the words were as soon as they left her mouth.

The three people that stood facing her hadn't come to the domes out of the goodness of their hearts. They'd come because the domes were paying them, or maybe even forcing them.

And now it's my job to make them help me harvest food that's better than anything they've eaten in their lives.

"I'm Nola." She held out a hand to the worker closest to her—an older woman about her mother's age, but with bright white, thinning hair.

"Catlyn." The woman's voice was low and soft as she took Nola's hand for only the briefest moment.

"Beauford," the only male in the group said, clasping his hands firmly behind his back as though daring Nola to force him to shake hands.

"Nice to meet you, Beauford." Nola nodded.

Beauford looked strong, healthy, and barely older than Nola herself. Aside from the wear on his clothes and faint rings under his eyes, he could have been from the domes.

For a moment, Nola forgot to breathe. What if the man was on Vamp? What if he had been injecting the drugs that were so popular in the city in order to stay healthy? But the domes would have blood-tested everyone they let in to work for illnesses that could be spread.

They must have checked for Vamp and Lycan as well.

"I'm T." The last worker's words pulled Nola back to the conversation, or lack thereof.

"T?" Nola asked.

The girl nodded with a forced and fleeting smile. Her long, auburn hair shimmered with the movement. Freckles covered the girl's face, and though she wore a long-sleeved, baggy shirt, Nola was sure that the freckles covered T's arms as well.

"I appreciate all of your help." Nola smiled as convincingly as she could. "First thing we need to do is harvest the tomatoes. Just pick the nice red ones—"

"We know what tomatoes are supposed to look like." Beauford grabbed a cart. "Just 'cause we're from the outside doesn't mean we're stupid."

"I never meant—" Nola began, but T shook her head.

"Don't worry about it, Miss. We know what we're here to do, let's just do it."

Without another word, the three outsiders began picking the tomatoes and laying them out on the carts. Nola moved far enough down the row to be able to glimpse one of the other work groups. The Domer in charge of the only other group in sight stood, hands on her hips, as she watched the outsiders work.

Lording over them as though they were animals that couldn't be trusted.

Nola walked back to her group and knelt on the sun-warmed earth, picking tomatoes and laying them on T's cart. T eyed her for a moment before continuing her work, carefully removing each good fruit.

It took hours to work their way down the line. By the time all the tomatoes had been harvested, they had five full carts, and the time for lunch had come.

A table had been brought out near the side of the dome, filled with food and vats of water.

"Right," Nola said, dusting her hands on her pants and hoping she was giving the right instructions. "We need to take the carts to the stairs, and then it'll be time for lunch."

At the word "lunch," all three outsiders turned toward the table laden with food. Nola's chest tightened at the look of hunger in their eyes.

A simple meal to us is something unbelievable to them.

Nola grabbed a cart and started pushing toward the stairs, not sure how to explain they would only be fed a simple work lunch.

Two of the other groups had already moved over to the food table. The supervisors sat off to one side, watching their charges eat the trays of fish and fruit they had been given.

Nola pushed her cart into line with those that held squash, beets, and kale. "I'll go back for the last cart." She turned to her crew.

They had formed a chain, Catlyn leading, Beauford in the middle, and T in the back, moving four carts between the three of them.

"Or...not," Nola said.

"We've got it," Catlyn said, her eyes on the table of food. As soon as the carts were in place, the three descended on the table, each taking a tray without looking at what was on them and settling onto the grass.

Nola surveyed the leftover trays. All had seared fish. It was the most abundant meat in the domes, so of course that's what they would feed the outsiders. Each piece of meat was accompanied by a handful of string beans and an apple, pear, or plum.

Nola chose a tray with a plum and sat down with her group. Each of them immediately stopped their ravenous eating to stare at her.

"May I join you?" she asked.

"Of course." Catlyn smiled then went back to eating at a slightly slower pace than before.

Beauford glanced at the other Domers in the corner with a look that clearly said he wished Nola had chosen to eat with her own kind.

Nola crunched a string bean, trying to think of something to say. She shouldn't ask about jobs. If they had those, they wouldn't be working in the domes. She shouldn't ask about family. With the child mortality rate on the outside so high, at least one of them would have lost a family member. "So how did you get chosen to work here?" was the first thing she could think to say that didn't seem too terribly offensive.

"You're right," Beauford said. "We were *chosen*. It is such an honor to harvest food we'll never eat."

"We are eating it." Catlyn glanced fearfully at Nola.

"They came around the city looking for folks," T said, looking Nola square in the eyes. "People who didn't have jobs and were still healthy, or at least not contagious. There weren't very many to choose from. I don't think anyone they found hasn't been brought to work in some capacity. Hauling glass for the walls or working on planting at least."

Nola froze, a string bean halfway to her mouth. "You're it? The ones who came to work are the only healthy ones left?"

"The ones who haven't turned to Lycan or Vamp," Beauford said.

"We're the only ones without jobs," T corrected, giving Beauford a hard look. "The healthy ones like us all work in factories or the few shops that haven't been trampled. Workers who won't cough blood on the machines or die on the floor are in huge demand."

"Then why aren't you working somewhere out there?" Nola tried to rid her mind of the image of a human coughing blood. She understood the reality of illness, but hearing T speak of it in such a matter-of-fact way somehow made it worse.

"There won't be factories in the city much longer." Catlyn reached over and squeezed T's hand. "Between the fires and the city falling to the Vampers and the wolves, and with those poor zombie folks attacking people in the streets, there isn't really a way for people to buy things."

"The only factories left are the ones making those nice uniforms you wear and extra glass for your walls." Beauford took a violent bite out of his apple.

"And even those are starting to shut down." T glanced sideways at the guards. "The fires a while ago took out a factory, and then the fighting at Nightland took out another. That's how we lost our jobs. You'll still have new glass and machines, but don't expect clothes to be coming in from the city for much longer. Destroying Nightland hurt the city, too."

"Nightland," Nola said, focusing hard on T's eyes to keep her head from spinning. "Getting rid of Vampers hurt the city?"

"It hurt a lot of people," T said.

"There were some factories that were damaged," Catlyn said. "We were right above the tunnels, and when the guards went in, part of our floor collapsed. The machines stopped working, and we didn't have the parts to fix them."

"But Nightland was in a Vamper neighborhood," Nola said. "How could a factory have been hurt?"

"Nightland reached under the streets and touched more of the city than you would ever know, Nola Kent." T leaned in, her eyes boring into Nola's.

The sound of her last name echoed in Nola's ears.

She knows. She knows who I am! The voice in her head screamed. Wouldn't stop screaming. Her breath hitched in her chest as panic set in.

No. No, stop it. She dug her fingers into the grass, willing the world not to slip away from her. *Someone said my name in front of her. My mother, another Domer. They told her I would be in charge of her group.*

"It is an honor to help the domes." Catlyn's voice reemerged as the pounding in Nola's ears quieted.

Catlyn smiled brightly and put a hand on T's shoulder, pulling her away from Nola. "They are offering us good pay and a good lunch. I've never actually eaten a piece of fruit like this." Catlyn held up her pear. "It really is delicious."

"I'm glad you like it." Nola stared down at the food on her plate, suddenly too disgusted to eat.

"We should get back to work." Beauford stood, his plate already clean.

Nola nodded, leaving her mostly full plate on the ground.

"Aren't you going to eat that?" Catlyn eyed Nola's food.

Nola shook her head. Before she could say she really wasn't hungry, Catlyn had snatched the plate, pushing the extra food onto T's.

"I don't need—" T began.

"You'll eat and be happy about it," Catlyn said.

"Yes, ma'am," T murmured, eating Nola's leftover lunch in a few quick bites.

The whole thing was over before Nola could think.

"Time to move the plants?" Catlyn gave Nola a bright smile as she pulled T to her feet. "What sort of plants are they going to be adding in? Something exotic maybe?"

"I don't know." Nola looked up at her mother who still stood on the platform in the middle of the dome. "They'll let me know when we get that far."

CHAPTER SIX

Trimming back the dead plants took another hour. Then the delicate process of digging up the roots began. The living vines had to be cut loose from the trellises. Once the roots were free, everything had to be shifted down the row.

Nola lifted the first of the root bases, her arms burning with the weight of it.

T crouched down to lift the next one.

"Don't," Beauford said, taking T under the arms and lifting her to her feet. "You keep the vine part from dragging."

"I can do it," T said so softly Nola almost couldn't hear.

"But we won't let you," Catlyn whispered, looking at the ground as soon as she noticed Nola watching them.

"Coming," Beauford said, easily lifting the root bundle and following Nola the twenty feet down the row to where the plants needed to be transferred.

Nola settled her roots into the freshly dug and perfectly sized hole. T trailed behind her, supporting the delicate vine.

"Are you hurt?" Nola asked, glancing around to make sure none of the other Domers heard her. If Lenora knew T couldn't lift, she would be taken out of the domes and sent back to the rubble of the factory Nightland had destroyed.

"No, Miss," T said.

"Because if you are," Nola said, reaching out and taking T's sleeve, her body making the decision before her mind could reason through her action, "you can tell me. I won't tell them, they won't get rid of you."

"It's got nothing to do with you," Beauford said, stepping in front of T.

He bumped Nola backward, but she still had a grip on T's sleeve. Her slight tug on the fabric lifted the waist of the shirt, revealing T's swollen stomach.

"I-I'm," Nola stuttered, letting go of T's shirt. "I'm sorry. I didn't know."

"You weren't supposed to." T pulled the baggy shirt down, covering her stomach.

"But if you're pregnant, you shouldn't be doing this kind of work," Nola whispered, searching the rows to make sure no one could hear.

"If I don't work, how am I supposed to eat?" T said.

"Women on the outside do heavy work all the time while they're carrying," Catlyn said, taking Beauford's arm and moving him out of the way before he could speak again.

"But you need to be careful," Nola said.

"Don't you think the Domers who brought us in here knew?" T asked. "They're willing to let me work, so let's just get to it before they think I'm slowing things down."

T held the vines up, waiting for Nola to tie them to the trellis.

"Fine," Nola whispered, pulling thick twine from her pocket and carefully attaching the vines, "but you don't do heavy lifting, and if you start feeling sick, you tell me."

"I'm an outsider," T said, her face unreadable. "*Sick* is a very relative term for us."

Nola opened her mouth to argue, but before she could think

of anything to say, a wail rent the air, shaking her lungs and stinging her ears.

The domes' sirens blared, and red lights flashed overhead.

Nola ran toward the glass, stumbling over the freshly dug holes in the ground. Heart racing, she searched the world outside for explosions and attackers. But there were no Vampers charging the domes. No bright orange flames destroying her home.

"Everyone evacuate now!" Lenora's voice carried over the siren. "Nola!"

She turned to see her mother running toward her, arms outstretched.

"Nola!"

"We have to go!" Nola shouted to Catlyn, Beauford, and T. "Come with me!"

The three hesitated for only a moment before following Nola as she ran toward her mother.

"Nola!" Lenora grabbed her hand, and together they ran down the stairs. The other work groups had beaten them down the steps, leaving only the guards in the dome.

"What's going on?" Nola asked as soon as they were down in the concrete corridor. The sound of the siren was different here, echoing down the hall in a more menacing way than it had sounded in the open space of the Amber Dome.

"Trouble in the city," one of the guards said. "All civilians are to report to the bunkers."

"What?"

Before the guard could answer Nola, her mother had dragged her down the hall.

"This way!" Nola turned to call to her group, but the guards had stopped them in the hall, herding them with the other outsiders.

"Where are they taking them?" she asked. "Mom, where are they taking the workers?"

"Not our problem." Lenora sped up to a run as they joined the throng of Domers heading toward the bunker.

Two bunkers had been built to protect the people of the domes. One underneath the atrium and one underneath seed storage. While the atrium had been badly damaged in the Nightland attack, the bunker was buried too deep to have been harmed. Even still, instinct and fear drove all the dome residents toward the seed storage bunker.

The scream of the sirens didn't lessen as Nola followed the crowd deeper underground. The weight of the earth above pressed down on her lungs, stifling her breath.

"What's happening?" Nola repeated the question to everyone she got close to, hoping one of them might have an answer. If there was trouble in the city all the way across the river, why should the Domers have to hide? There were fights in the city all the time and riots every few weeks. But never before had the residents of the domes been sent into the bunkers.

Nola had only ever gone into the bunkers during the biannual emergency drills. She hadn't made it down that far when Nightland attacked.

But this was no drill. Panic permeated the air. When they reached the barracks level, a long line of Outer Guard ran past in full riot gear. Thick jackets with armored vests, screened helmets, and shining pistols made the guards one congruous, and terrifying, unit.

Jeremy would be with them, racing toward whatever terrible thing might be happening.

"Jeremy!" Nola fought to free herself from the ever-moving crowd. But she couldn't escape the throng. "Jeremy!" Before she made it to the hall where the Outer Guard had been passing, they disappeared up the steps, the gap closing behind them.

Nola let the crowd sweep her the rest of the way to the bunker. Guards held the thick steel door open, waiting for the last of the Domers to make it through.

"Keep moving in!" the guard shouted as Nola passed.

The crowd had stopped right inside the doorway, leaving no room for the rest of the people to file in.

"All the way to the back!" a voice ordered, and the crowd began to move.

A man much taller than Nola stood right in front of her. The people behind her forced her forward, pressing her face into the man's back.

She tipped her head up toward the ceiling, focusing on the caged light bulbs and flashing red beams.

Breathe in. Breathe out. Breathe in.

Jeremy will be going into the city.

Breathe out.

Jeremy will be fighting, and I'll be locked underground.

Tears crept into the corners of Nola's eyes as the thick metal door slammed shut.

CHAPTER SEVEN

"Find a place and calm down!" a gravelly voice shouted.

The crowd spread, moving toward the benches and tables that lined the walls. Above the tables hung metal rectangles that could be folded down into makeshift beds.

Please don't let us still be trapped here when it's time to sleep.

As people began to sit, she scanned the crowd for her mother. Lenora glowered by the door, grilling the guard who had shut them in.

"Has seed storage been locked down?" Lenora asked, her tone reflecting the importance of protecting the seeds. Without the seeds, there was no point in hiding in the bunker. The Domers would just starve to death.

"We told you last time," the guard said, "seed storage was locked down before we even came down to the bunker. The seeds are as safe as we are."

"I should be allowed to stay with my seeds," Lenora spoke through gritted teeth.

"All dome residents have to come to the bunkers," the guard said. "I'm sorry, Ms. Kent, but the Council made that quite clear. They are unwilling to take any more chances with dome citizen lives. If you want them to change the rules, you'll have to talk to the Council about it. Which should be easy since you're on the Council."

"Don't take that cheek with me," Lenora said. "Why have they put us down here in the first place?"

Nola inched closer to her mother, gazing aimlessly around the bunker while listening to the guard speak, afraid if he caught her eavesdropping he might not tell Lenora the truth.

"There's a fight in the city," the guard said, his voice low. "A big one. And it's not just in one place, it's all over. The radio said it was like an all-out street war."

"War between whom?" Lenora asked. "It's daylight, and the Vampers of Nightland all fled. The filthy, thieving, murdering cowards."

"I have no idea, ma'am. I honestly don't," the guard said. "I'm only doing as I'm told. I only know what the radio's told me. The only thing any of us in here can do is wait for word and try to keep everyone calm. So please, Ms. Kent, sit down and relax. As soon as I hear anything, I promise you'll be the first to know."

"I'd better be," Lenora growled before turning to Nola.

"Come along, Magnolia." Lenora took Nola's elbow and led her to the front bench.

Every seat had already been filled by fearful people who spoke in hushed tones.

"I'm so sorry, but we're going to need to sit here," Lenora said. "I need to stay by the door." It was a sign of how frightening Lenora was that all five people on the bench stood without argument and walked down the bunker without so much as an angry look over their shoulders.

"We could have gone farther back." Nola sat next to her mother. "The guard could have found you."

"But here I can watch him," Lenora said, her eyes fixed on the guard. "If he hears anything in his earpiece, I'll know."

Nola nodded, though she knew her mother couldn't see her.

Two little girls sat across from them with their mother and father. Nola studied the children, hoping that memorizing the blonde curls on the girls' heads would keep the horrible nightmares from coming.

It doesn't count as a nightmare if I'm awake.

That one errant thought allowed the images to whirl into being. Her father, dressed in an Outer Guard's uniform, going to stop a Vamper riot in the city and coming home covered in a plain white sheet Nola wasn't allowed to look beneath.

She hadn't understood the fighting then. Hadn't known what the screaming and terrible banging would sound like. In Nightland, she had heard the screams when the Outer Guard had blown their way in. The dust roughly coating her throat, and the horrible wailing ringing in her ears.

When Nightland attacked, it had been worse. So much worse. Glass had shattered, and blood slicked the floor. The world stained red, breaking every promise of safety. Maybe that's why they had all been sent so far beneath the surface. With the Outer Guard in the city, the domes were vulnerable. The domes couldn't afford to lose any more people. There had already been too much blood and death.

Nola's breath caught in her chest.

"You're all right, Magnolia." Lenora squeezed her daughter's hand. "Take a deep breath. That's all you have to do to stay calm."

I wish that were true.

Five hours passed before the guard at the door lifted his hand, pressing his fingers to his earpiece. His brow wrinkled for a moment, and before it looked like he had finished listening, Lenora shot to her feet, ready to question the poor man.

Nola glanced back at the rest of the bunker. Some people had already pulled beds down from the walls, but most still sat on the benches, talking quietly to their neighbors or staring silently at the walls.

Lenora's movement drew the attention of those nearest her. Silently, Nola followed her mother.

"What's going on?" Lenora asked in a hushed tone.

"They're coming back from the city." The guard held up a hand when it looked like Lenora was going to ask another question. "That's really all I know."

"Is anyone hurt?" Nola asked, dropping any pretense she wasn't listening.

"Yes." Fear touched the guard's eyes. "All medical personnel please come to the front of the bunker!" the guard shouted, his voice resonating through the concrete space. It was big enough to fit all the residents of the dome, but the hard walls allowed his voice to reverberate loudly enough for everyone to hear.

The medical personnel sprinted to the door. Sound burst out around the bunker, people shouting to know what had happened, who needed help.

"Silence!" the guard bellowed. "Only medical personnel will be allowed out now. That is the only information I have. Everyone else, please stay seated."

He punched a code into a panel at the side of the door, and the metal bolt slid aside. The medical personnel ran up the hall, but Lenora stepped in front of the guard when he tried to close the door.

"If it is safe enough for them to work on patients, it is safe enough for me to check on my seeds."

"Ms. Kent—"

"Dr. Kent," Lenora corrected.

Neither of them noticed Nola standing only a foot away. Without any thought of consequences, she darted through the door and up the stairs, following the line of medical staff.

Jeremy had gone out into the city. If he was hurt, she had to be with him.

She slowed to a walk.

Be with him and do what? You aren't a doctor.

Nola took a breath, letting the calm of the hall fill her. The sirens had stopped blaring. The only noise was the fading sound of footfalls as the doctors ran toward their patients.

You need to get to Jeremy, because he would find a way to get to you.

She didn't run up the stairs. Instead, she looked carefully around each corner, making sure she didn't meet anyone who would try to send her away.

She didn't see another person until she reached the tunnel level. Guards tore through the halls, carrying stretchers that bore their injured comrades. Doctors ran between patients, assessing the ones who needed the most immediate treatment.

Dome Guard were mixed in with Outer Guard.

They took all of them into the city.

Nola pressed herself to the wall, trying to catch a glimpse of Jeremy. Or better yet, hear his strong healthy voice giving an order. But she didn't see him. He was tall enough that his dirty-blond hair should have been visible above the crowd. Unless he was one of the ones who kept their helmet on.

Gentry Ridgeway came into view, carrying a stretcher with an older black-haired man lying unconscious on it. Trying to walk as though she was meant to be there, Nola started out into the hall, following Gentry, hoping she would know where her younger brother might be.

"Out of the way," a guard barked as he ran past the others. The guard on his stretcher gasped rattling breaths. Blood stained one side of his chest, and the mark grew wider every second. One of his arms had been severed at the elbow. The sight of raw flesh sent bile into Nola's throat.

Jeremy. Find Jeremy.

Nola staggered down the hall, following Gentry, ignoring someone's warning of, "Miss, you need to get out of here!"

Most of the gurneys had been brought into the largest medical room. Screams of pain and shouted orders filled the air. Nola staggered as the stench of blood and chemicals slammed her in the face.

No longer caring about being caught, Nola tore down the row, searching for Jeremy. But none of the people in the room wore Outer Guard uniforms.

"Where are the Outer Guard?" Nola grabbed the arm of a Dome Guard. "Where did they take them?"

"Next level down, to the barracks," the guard said, not seeming to care that Nola shouldn't be there. Even though the guard had been carrying others, blood seeped out of a gash on his thigh.

"You need help." Nola reached toward the guard.

"We all need help." The guard limped back out to the hall.

Running the length of the room, Nola went out the far door, cutting down the corridor to avoid the doctors and taking a longer route to the stairs.

The sounds coming from the lower level were different from those of the medical area. There were no screams of pain or panic. The Outer Guard were groomed to stay calm no matter what, but the lack of sound shot more terror through Nola than the screaming had.

She ran down the stairs, but before she was three steps into the hall, a hand reached out and grabbed her.

"Nola, what are you doing here?" Blood streaked Gentry's face and matted her blonde hair.

"Jeremy," Nola said. "Where is he? Is he okay?"

Gentry's eyes flicked to the door behind Nola for a split second. "Nola, he'll be fine. They're taking care of him."

"Is he hurt?" Panic surged in her chest. "What happened?"

"Nola, you have to get out of here."

Two women carried another stretcher down the stairs. The guard at the front pushed Gentry and Nola aside, not seeming to care if she knocked them over. Gentry's grip on Nola's arm slackened for only a moment, but it was enough. Nola yanked her arm free and ran toward the door Gentry's eyes had flicked to, hoping it would be the right one.

Nola shoved open the swinging door and froze.

Jeremy, lying on a table, covered in blood. His own blood. Doctors moved around him, one of them giving orders to the others.

One ripped away the tattered shreds of uniform that covered Jeremy's stomach.

"No!" Nola screamed without realizing the word had left her mouth, but the doctors didn't notice the noise.

Ragged gashes cut deep into the flesh of Jeremy's stomach. Blood poured from a bullet-shaped hole in the center of his chest.

Jeremy's face was untouched; his helmet had protected him. His eyes were closed, he could have been sleeping.

"What the hell are you doing in here?" A doctor knocked Nola aside, a needle filled with black liquid held in her hand. "Someone get her the hell out of here!"

An arm seized Nola around the waist, lifting her out of the room. She didn't turn to see who it was. She couldn't look away from Jeremy as the doctor rammed the needle into his chest.

"Nola, I told you to get out of here!" Gentry grabbed Nola by the shoulders and shook her. "Nola! You have to leave!"

"Jeremy." Nola swayed on the spot. "Not Jeremy, please not Jeremy."

Sympathy flickered in Gentry's eyes. "He'll be fine, I promise you. My brother can make it through this. But you have to go before more people notice you're here."

"I can't leave him." Nola tried to go back through the door. "He stayed with me in the hospital, I have to be with him."

"Later." Gentry dragged Nola away, dodging between stretchers and shouting guards. "If you care about my brother at all, you will run as far away as you can and pretend you were never here. If anyone asks you, lie." Gentry grabbed Nola's chin and looked straight into her eyes. "Nola Kent, you have to lie. Now go!"

Without another word, Gentry ran down the hall toward the stairs to the atrium. There were still more wounded coming down the steps. Most of them were on their feet now, being helped along by other guards. How many had been hurt?

All of them. All the guards.

Nola turned and ran down the hall in the opposite direction of the stairs. She couldn't bear to pass them. To look at their faces and not know if they would survive.

The Guard barracks made up the rest of the hall. She would find a place to hide, a place in the dark. A few of the wounded had been brought into the barracks, the ones who weren't as badly ripped and bleeding as Jeremy. Nola's breath hitched in her throat, and she ran farther, down to the end of the hall.

There was a thick door she had never thought to look at before, but she didn't hesitate as she reached for the handle. Didn't wonder when the heavy handle turned easily. Didn't stop to think until she had entered the long hallway that shouldn't have existed.

CHAPTER EIGHT

The hallway was narrow. Nola noticed that first. It was long, too. Over a hundred feet. One hundred feet of tunnel that shouldn't exist. That *didn't* exist on the domes' maps. The Guard barracks should have been the last thing on this level. But the long corridor stretched out in front of her.

With a *swish*, the door to the barracks closed. The noise of the guards disappeared. Nola stood frozen for a moment, waiting for Gentry to grab her and shout that she wasn't supposed to be here either. Even without Gentry yelling at her, the air told her this wasn't a place she was allowed to be. Doors lined the hall. Thick, metal doors with tiny windows at the top.

Fists clenched, Nola took a step forward, then another, walking toward the nearest door.

The window was nearly too high for her to see through. Rising up on her toes, she peered into the room beyond. Six bunks hung along the back and side walls. People rested on the bunks. Nola ducked as Catlyn pushed herself up on her elbow, staring toward the window.

Carefully, Nola reached for the door handle and tried to turn it. The door was locked tight.

They left the workers locked in.

Fear mingled with rage in her chest. Those people were from the city. Their families might have been hurt, and they were locked up.

But they locked all the Domers up, too.

Slowly, Nola peered back through the window. Catlyn lay back on her bunk. T had taken the bed beneath her, lying on her side, one hand draped across her stomach. Beauford was nowhere to be seen. Only women had been locked in this room.

Nola tiptoed across the hall, peeking into the cell opposite. Men filled this room, but they weren't lying on their beds. The men sat on their bunks, talking to each other, saying things she couldn't hear. One of the men glanced toward the window, making eye contact with Nola for a split second before she dodged out of sight. The sound of fists banging on the door echoed through the hall.

"Let us out of here, you filthy Domer!" The thick metal muffled the angry voice. "We didn't agree to be your captives! You're worse than the monsters on the streets! At least they don't lie about what they are!"

Nola leaned against the wall, her heart racing in her chest. They would let them out as soon as the threat was over, they would have to. Nola wanted to look back through the glass, to explain the domes meant them no harm, but she couldn't risk him recognizing her later.

What if I'm wrong? What if the guards don't let them out of the cells as soon as the danger is gone?

She crept farther down the hall. There were two more rooms on either side, all four the same size as the ones closest to the door, all four holding six outsiders. Six more closely spaced doors waited beyond the filled cells. Nola stayed on one side of the hall, looking through each of the windows as she passed. These rooms were empty. In each of them a single ledge of stone, which looked as though it were meant to be a bed, stuck out of the wall, and a crude sink and toilet were securely set into the concrete.

"At least they didn't lock you in there," Nola whispered, wishing the man who had screamed at her could see the guards had put him in the better place.

Moving across to the other side, she glanced into each cell. When she finally got to the last window in the hall, she sighed at the unoccupied bed, relieved for a moment the guards hadn't been cruel enough to lock the outsiders up with only stone to sleep on. But then her eyes caught a glimpse of color on the floor.

Scarlet and purple atop a figure dressed all in black lying curled up on the ground. Slowly, the figure moved.

Run.

Her body shouted at her to flee, but her feet clung to the concrete as a pair of black eyes met her gaze.

Raina.

Her face was paler than even a vampire's should be. She'd been stripped of the leather clothes Nola had always seen her wear and dressed in a black cotton hospital gown that hung open in the back.

Raina's hair hung limp around her face as she pushed herself shakily to her feet, her eyes not drifting from Nola's face. Mouse-brown roots showed through the streaks of scarlet and purple in her hair.

Raina lurched toward the door, stumbling and thudding against the metal. She was taller than Nola, tall enough that she could look easily through the window, her face only inches from Nola's.

"You're alive," Nola whispered, fear and relief mixed in her voice.

Raina stared at her.

"I thought you were dead," Nola said as loudly as she dared.

Raina rolled her eyes. Even that slight movement looked as

though it cost more energy than Raina could spare. "You would think that, wouldn't you?"

"You were stabbed in the chest." Nola's hands trembled at the memory of it. The man trying to drink from Nola's throat, Raina saving her. Raina jumping in front of a knife to save Nola...again. "I thought it killed you."

"He didn't get my heart, Domer." Raina sneered, swaying as she continued. "Though if I'd known this would be my fate, I would have stabbed myself in the heart. Or cut off my head. I'm not too picky."

"How long have you been in here?" Nola glanced down the hall. She still couldn't hear anything from the barracks beyond. What if they had more people they wanted to add to the cells?

"How long ago was the rebellion?" Raina asked.

"Rebellion?" Nola's voice rose in anger. "You mean the time you broke into the domes and murdered innocent people?"

"Innocence is in the eye of the beholder." Raina gave a weary shrug, like the thought of dead Domers meant nothing to her.

"You destroyed our home," Nola said. "You stole from us!"

"We took what we needed to survive."

"Well, I hope you have a great time surviving in here." Nola turned to leave.

"Because I got captured after getting stabbed to save your damned life?" Raina's crackling voice echoed through the hall. "Yeah, I'll try."

"Don't pretend you saved me because you actually like me." Nola smacked both hands hard against the door, taking pleasure in Raina's flinch. "You saved me because Emanuel told you to. And I don't even know why he bothered to do that. Did it make him feel better about destroying my home?"

"If you think this is what a *destroyed home* looks like, you know even less than I thought you did, little girl." Raina turned and sagged back to her spot on the floor. "And it wasn't Emanuel who cared enough to want you to stay alive. It was Kieran. Your precious Kieran. I guess I deserve to be locked up in this florescent-lit, concrete hell for listening to a lovesick kid. Now leave me the fuck alone. I saved your life, at least let me die slowly in peace."

Raina curled back up, her face hidden beneath the curtain of her hair.

Nola slid down the door and pressed her forehead into the cool metal, taking deep, shuddering breaths, willing herself not to panic.

Kieran had protected her. Told the others not to hurt her. She jammed her hands in her hair, pulling hard against the roots. He had wanted to keep her safe. She had to be safe, but everyone in the domes that she loved could die. Her home could be shattered, her family killed, but he wanted her alive.

It was cruel.

"He wanted to torture me." Nola viciously wiped away the tears on her face. "That is not love, Nola Kent. If Kieran loved you..." She choked on the words. It didn't matter if Kieran had ever loved her. His betrayal was too much to ever forgive.

And Jeremy...wonderful, steady Jeremy who had forgiven her, or at least wanted to, was hurt and bleeding and she couldn't help him. She couldn't help anyone.

Shaking so hard she could barely stand, Nola fought her way to her feet. She wouldn't stay near Raina. And there was no point hiding in here anyway. She would have to leave the hall eventually, might as well be caught now. She would lie to the guards, say she had never seen Jeremy's terrible wounds.

Another lie to add to the ever-growing list.

Slowly, she walked down the hall. Trying not to think of the innocent people who were still locked behind metal doors, hoping the guards really would let them out as soon as the domes were safe.

Nola opened the door to the barracks hall and stepped forward. There were still doctors running between rooms,

treating patients. There were still no screams of pain or fear from the Outer Guard, only the precision of orders immediately obeyed. The ten minutes she had been gone really hadn't changed the scene that much. The doctors had moved on to other patients, and there were no more stretchers being carried down the stairs. But smears of blood still marred the floor.

She looked at the door through which Jeremy lay, wanting to walk in and shout that she was staying with him and there was nothing they could do to stop her. But Gentry had said to go. Gentry had promised Jeremy would be all right if Nola left. She walked up the stairs, not daring to look back for fear she wouldn't keep going.

She had to trust Gentry to tell her the truth and Jeremy to heal. She had to trust the guards would let the outsiders go as soon as it was safe and keep Raina where she couldn't hurt anyone.

If I can't trust the domes, there's nothing left for me to hold onto.

Nola turned away from the hospital corridor at the top of the stairs, heading back down the hall to Bright Dome. She shuddered at the sounds of the wounded Dome Guard, but two long corridors later, the noise faded away. Only the steady rhythm of her footsteps ruined the calm of the hall. The others must still be in the bunker below.

Large letters marked the wall: *Bright Dome.* Nola traced the letters with her finger. Home. Bright Dome was her home. She wouldn't be able to get back into the bunker anyway. And her mother would be locked in her lab with the seeds by now.

She walked the rest of the way to her house in a daze. Examining every tree she passed. Trying to memorize the shape of each stone on the path that led her home. Counting the steps it took her to reach her room. The purple-spotted orchid sat on her desk. Jeremy's wonderful gift.

Even thinking his name sent panic surging through her chest. He had to be okay. There was no other choice. Nola climbed onto her windowsill and reached up. Her arms burned as she pulled herself onto the soft moss that covered the roof. She lay down, burying her face in the damp, earthy smell, and screamed. Tears burned in her eyes, and a sob ripped through her chest.

"No!" Nola growled, hating the tears that poured down her cheeks. "No, no, no," she whimpered as panic overwhelmed her.

Curling up on her side under the dark sky, she sobbed. Alone under the glass.

CHAPTER NINE

The sun had already peeked over the horizon when voices from the ground woke Nola. She couldn't make out any words in the sleepy murmurs but blinking away the clouds her tears had left behind, dozens of shapes appeared in the dim light. People making their way home. She rubbed her eyes, feeling their swelling under her fingers.

She watched the group move, waiting for her mother to come toward their house. But Lenora wasn't with them. Digging her fingers into the moss, Nola climbed back through her window and crept to her mother's room. It was empty, as was the rest of the house. Nola stood in the pale darkness.

A void had swallowed her whole. Her tears had dried up. But she had thought that before. When her father died, when Kieran was banished, when the domes were attacked. But it wasn't true. Tears couldn't dry up forever, just until the next terrible thing happened.

Nola walked out the kitchen door and into the dome, brushing her fingers over her curls to get rid of the bits of moss that clung to her from sleeping on the roof.

More people filtered into Bright Dome as she walked down the stairs.

Jeremy.

If people were coming into the domes, it should be safe for her to go and see Jeremy. Breaking into a run, Nola sprinted through the corridors, ignoring the sleepy glares of the people she dodged past.

Through the corridors and down the stairs, no one tried to stop her until she reached the barracks level.

"You can't come down here, Miss." An Outer Guard stepped in front of Nola, holding out a hand to block her path.

"Jeremy Ridgeway," Nola said. "I know he was hurt, and I want to see him."

Pain and sympathy creased the guard's brow.

"He's okay." Nola's voice shook. "Please tell me he's okay."

"He's alive," the guard said, "but I don't have authorization to let you see him."

"Ask Captain Ridgeway," Nola begged, letting the news that Jeremy was, in fact, alive embolden her. "He'll say I can see him. I promise, I'll wait here."

The guard stared at Nola before waving another guard over. The woman limped as she approached. "Ask Captain Ridgeway if Magnolia Kent can see Jeremy."

The other guard nodded and limped away toward Captain Ridgeway's office.

It's not that bad. If his dad's not with him, it can't be that bad.

But the blood and the terrible wounds.

"How did you know my name?" Nola asked, seizing the only thing her mind could cling to aside from Jeremy being so terribly hurt.

"You're the one the Vampers captured," the guard said. "We sent a crew into the city after you, organized a whole mission to find you. I was on the failed rescue mission in Nightland. It's hard to forget a face you go into battle for, especially if you fail to save the person you're after."

An all too familiar shadow passed across the guard's face.

"You didn't fail," Nola whispered. "I'm here, aren't I?"

The guard nodded and gave a pinched smile.

"The captain said she can go in." The limping guard returned. "But she's not to wake Ridgeway or disturb the wound dressings."

Wound dressings.

Nola exhaled shakily. "I just want to see him."

The limping guard nodded and beckoned for Nola to follow her. "He's a lucky guy. Keep a good watch on him for us."

"I will," Nola said, so softly her words barely made a sound as the door to Jeremy's room swung open.

He lay on a bed, needles and tubes attached to his arm. He slept peacefully, no pain marring his face nor any trace of blood on the white gown that covered him.

Nola walked toward Jeremy, not noticing the guard had followed her into the room until she pulled up a chair for Nola to sit next to the bed. Before Nola could thank her, she slipped back out, leaving her and Jeremy alone in the room.

The white gown and sheet of the bed couldn't diminish Jeremy. He didn't look smaller or weaker. Only peaceful. If it hadn't been for the tubes in his arms, he could have simply fallen asleep after a long day of work in the domes.

She watched his chest rise and fall with each breath. No rattle came from the terrible hole that had pierced him. She reached for his hand before stopping herself. She wasn't to wake him. Instead, she curled up on the chair and stared at him.

The tiny lines from his constant smile showed even in sleep. But the newer lines, the ones made by worry, were gone. He hadn't shaved in a few days. Stubble marked his chin. Nola wanted to touch his cheeks. To feel their roughness on her skin. To feel the warmth that meant life still filled him.

Wrapping her arms around herself, she fought the urge to hold him. Trying to content herself with watching his chest rise and fall, rise and fall. Each breath was another victory. Another moment of life the cruel outside world hadn't stolen from them.

Inhale, exhale. Inhale, exhale.

How many millions of breaths would mean they had made it through another year?

Inhale, exhale.

How many breaths until it counted as a long, full life?

She didn't know she had fallen asleep until fingers grazed her palm.

"Nola," a gravelly voice whispered.

She blinked, trying to see in the dim light of the room. A hand lay gently in hers.

"Nola," the voice said again. She looked up to Jeremy. His eyes were open, and a faint smile curved his lips. "Are you all right?"

She choked on her laugh, tears tightening her throat. "Am I all right?" Nola repeated, tenderly twining her fingers through his. "You almost died, and you're asking if I'm all right?"

"Always." Jeremy reached toward her.

"Don't." Nola moved closer as a shadow of pain crossed Jeremy's face. She leaned in, kissing his palm and pressing it to her cheek. "You have to stay still and rest so you can heal."

"I'll heal just fine." Jeremy grinned. Only his eyes betrayed his pain and fatigue. "I just want to hold you."

"If your dad thinks you aren't resting because I'm here, he'll kick me out." She glanced toward the door. "I don't want to leave."

"Come up here then." Jeremy patted the bed next to him. "Then I can hold you without moving."

"I don't want to hurt you. You were wounded in the city. Really, really badly and..." She didn't have the words to say how close to losing him they had come.

"I know." He took her hand, coaxing her toward the bed. "I

was there, and it hurt like hell. But I'm going to be fine. And I'll sleep a lot better if I can feel you safe beside me."

She sat gently on the bed, easing her weight down slowly and watching his face for any sign she was causing him pain.

"I was safe, you know." Nola lay down next to Jeremy. He drew her in so her head rested on his shoulder. "I was in a bunker. You were the one out fighting."

"It doesn't matter where you are, Nola." He kissed the top of her head. "I'm always going to worry about you. I love you too much not to."

"I love you, too." She tipped her chin up and brushed her lips against his. "You have to rest and get better. I need you whole and healthy."

"I'll be fine." He smiled, and this time his joy touched his eyes as well. "As long as I've got you."

"Sleep," she whispered. "I'll be here when you wake up. I promise."

"Don't let them make you leave," Jeremy said, and in a moment, he was asleep.

Closing her eyes, she could feel the steady rise and fall of his chest as it timed with her own breaths.

He was alive, and he loved her.

I love him.

A smile still on her lips, Nola drifted to sleep.

___

CHAPTER TEN

___

Lights flashed on. With a squeak, Nola fell, thudding onto the concrete floor.

"Nola!" Jeremy shouted.

"I'm fine," she groaned.

"Sorry to wake you," Captain Ridgeway said from his place by the door. While he didn't look sorry, he didn't look angry either, which Nola took to be a good sign as she pushed herself off the floor. "The doctors are ready to check on you, Jeremy."

The captain stepped aside, letting a doctor dressed in a white uniform enter the room. The tag on the front of her uniform read *Doctor Mullins*.

"I feel great," Jeremy said, taking Nola's hand in his as soon as she stood.

"I need to check your wounds, nonetheless." Doctor Mullins glanced at Nola before looking back at Captain Ridgeway.

"Nola, if you wouldn't mind leaving while the doctor examines Jeremy." Captain Ridgeway held the door to the hall open.

"Sure." Nola started for the door, but Jeremy held tightly onto her hand.

"I don't need to be examined," Jeremy said. "I'm fine, and Nola can stay."

"You are an Outer Guard," Captain Ridgeway said, his voice leaving no doubt that he was speaking as Jeremy's commander, not his father. "You were wounded in the line of duty, and you will receive medical treatment."

"I'll wait outside." Nola kissed Jeremy's cheek. "I'll come back as soon as they're done."

Nodding to Captain Ridgeway, she went out into the hall to wait. The brightness of the lights in the hall meant it was nearly midday.

All the tunnels were lit according to the time of day to ensure the people of the domes would stay attuned to the sun even while working underground. But the false brightness bore into Nola's eyes, a garish contrast to the soothing light of Jeremy's room.

Even the few hours Nola had slept made a huge difference. No hint remained that patients had been treated in the hall. No blood marked the floor. The scent of fear and fighting had left the air. The door to one of the long barrack's rooms swung open. Half the beds Nola could see were filled with sleeping Outer Guard. The other half were empty.

Were the beds empty because the guards with families were in their homes aboveground or already out working? Had more been lost in the city?

But it wasn't Jeremy. I didn't lose him.

Self-loathing welled in Nola's chest.

Is it so terrible to want the person I love alive?

"Nola." Captain Ridgeway stepped out of the door and stood next to her, following her gaze toward the empty beds. "We lost two."

She looked up at Captain Ridgeway and felt like a little girl again. As terrified and small as the night he had come to tell them her father had been killed in a riot.

"I'm so sorry," Nola said. Her words sounded hollow, unbearably inadequate.

It had been winter when her father died. The air in the domes had been chilly. She remembered staring at the goose bumps on her arms while the captain told her mother how brave her father had been. How his act of heroism had saved lives. But all Nola could think was how badly she wanted her father brought back inside where it was warm. She didn't want him to sleep in the cold. Even if he was to sleep forever.

"What happened?" Nola asked, not really expecting an answer.

Captain Ridgeway rubbed his chin for a moment before speaking. "Follow me."

Without looking to see if she obeyed, he turned and strode down the hall to his office. Before she could take a step, he held the door open for her.

Feeling as though she were being led to a teacher's office for disobedience, Nola walked down the hall and through the open door.

It was a small room with only a desk, two chairs, and a filing cabinet. One picture sat on the desk. Jeremy and Gentry smiling together, back when Jeremy was shorter than his older sister. A faint hum permeated the air but did nothing to lessen the horrible quiet while Nola waited for the captain to speak. She expected him to sit behind his desk or offer her a chair, but he stayed just inside the door, standing right in front of her so she had to look up to see his face.

"It was the wolf packs. Since Nightland cleared out, there's been fighting to see who controls the city. Vampers don't naturally like to live together. A community like Nightland may very well have been the only one of its kind in the world. Now they're out of the city, and there isn't another Vamper group to step in and take power." Captain Ridgeway ran his calloused hands over the graying stubble on his face. "At least not one that can stand up to the wolf packs. The packs started by picking off Vampers, and now they've moved on to fighting each other to see who will end up in power."

"But why did all the guards go into the city?" she asked, unsure if she had overstepped by speaking. "I know the Outer Guard have to protect the peace in the city, but the Dome Guard have never gone in to stop riots."

"We aren't dealing with riots. It's become an all-out street war. They aren't burning factories, they're burning homes. Taking over whole blocks, and anyone who tries to fight back, or just doesn't run fast enough, dies. Or is forced to join the pack. So, the winning pack gets stronger and stronger—"

"Until they're as strong as Nightland and can come for us," Nola said. "So, you took everyone to try and stop the pack from growing. Did it work?"

"It bought us time," Captain Ridgeway said, "but we didn't stop them. I think the world might have fallen too far for us to actually keep the shadows from spreading."

Fear swelled in her chest. "Then what do we do?"

"Find a way to survive the shadows. Then fight like hell when they come to our door."

"We can't leave the domes." Nola's mind flipped through a hundred possibilities, trying to find a path that didn't lead to more gray smoke rising above the domes. "The food and the plants, they can't be moved. Even if we could find another place for the people."

"We aren't going to leave, we're going to fight. We'll burn the whole damn city if that's what it takes."

Nola froze, frightened by Captain Ridgeway's vehemence.

"I hope—" Nola searched for words in the tangles of her mind. "I hope it won't come to that. But if it's the city or the domes..."

"Then the domes have to survive. We were built to protect the future of mankind. And that's what we'll do, no matter what it takes."

The captain's words hung heavy in the air.

"Why are you telling me this?" Nola asked, wanting to flee Captain Ridgeway's heavy gaze. It felt like he was searching her, trying to find some grain of information that would help the domes survive. But even if she hadn't sworn to Jeremy that she would lie, there was nothing she knew that could save them from a wolf pack. "Isn't this the sort of thing the Outer Guard always try to hide from the rest of us?" she pressed on after a long moment of silence.

"It is," he said, "but for some reason you, Magnolia Kent, seem to be mired deeper in this bloody muck than the rest of us. And if there's one thing I've learned, it's that when blood and death come for someone once, they'll come back again. And again. The bloodthirsty don't forget."

The captain's words rang over her like a judge delivering a death sentence. She had played with shadows. Now she was condemned to darkness.

"They'll keep coming for me till they kill me." The words came so naturally, so simply, it felt like she had known since the first time she stared into the void of a Vamper's black eyes.

"They'll kill you, or you'll kill them. You can't get away from a monster that has your scent. And Emanuel isn't dead, at least not as far as we can tell. The storm that's brewing carries one word on the wind: *Nola*."

Nola swayed on the spot, and the captain caught her by the elbows.

"Your name is still spoken in the city. The second Nightland took you, you became a symbol of the domes. And until you're not, you aren't safe."

"Why are you telling me this?" she said, her voice stronger and louder in her anger as she pulled away from the captain. "If I'm doomed, why not just leave me in the streets and let the wolves have me? If Emanuel wants me, I'll go. I'm not worth more people dying. Just let it be done!"

"No. You are a citizen of the domes, and the Outer Guard are sworn to protect you. Letting the wolves have you wouldn't make the domes any safer. It would only make you dead. Not to mention my son is in love with you. And I'm not going to let the wolves or Vampers or zombies or whatever else this hellhole of a world throws at us destroy my son's life. He is willing to risk everything for you. It's my job to make sure that *everything* doesn't end up meaning his life."

"Tell me what to do." Her words came out as a plea. "Just tell me what I'm supposed to do."

"Stay safe, Magnolia. I don't know why you're so damned important, but you are. And if you end up in trouble again, my son will be running at the head of a pack of my guards trying to save you."

"I would never ask him to—" she couldn't form the words. "I want Jeremy to be safe."

"I'm glad we both agree on that." The captain's eyes darkened for a moment. "That's the problem with my raising children to be Outer Guard. They got to be really good at it."

"How was Jeremy hurt?" Nola pictured Jeremy running at the front of the guards as they fought the wolves, risking his life to protect everyone else's.

"The same as all Outer Guard get hurt." Captain Ridgeway opened the door to the hall. "Doing his duty to the domes." Without another word, he bowed Nola out of his office.

Nola jumped at the firm *click* of the door behind her as though it had been a gunshot. Part of her wanted to run as far away from the domes as it was possible for a person to go. Out into the wild where even the wolves and Vampers couldn't find her. But the much larger part wanted nothing more than to be with Jeremy. To make sure Doctor Mullins was positive he would to be all right.

Running toward the door, she knocked before anyone could try and stop her.

The instant Jeremy called, "Come in," she swung the door

open and slipped into the room, closing the door quickly and leaning against it, her heart racing as though she had just run from the boogeyman.

"I thought you'd run away." Jeremy sat up in bed and had more color in his cheeks than he'd had when he'd woken up.

"Your dad wanted to talk to me." Nola pushed herself off the door and ran the few steps to the bed, anxious to be closer to him. "Did the doctor say you could sit up? You need to be—"

"What did my dad want to talk to you about?" Jeremy cut her off, taking her hand and pulling her down to sit by his side.

"He told me—" Nola began, instinct telling her to lie, to say that Captain Ridgeway had lectured her about not tiring Jeremy and allowing him to rest and heal.

When did lying become so easy?

"He told me he's worried about me," she began again. "He thinks the wolves or Vampers or someone will come after me again. Apparently, I'm a symbol of what the outsiders hate about the domes, so basically I'm doomed. Mostly, I think he's worried you'll get hurt trying to protect me. I can't let anything happen to you because of me." She dug her nails into her palms to keep her hands from shaking.

"Don't worry about me getting hurt," Jeremy said, taking her hands in his. "Turns out I'm really pretty good at this guard thing."

She laughed weakly. "Good or not, I just want you to be safe."

"I will be." Jeremy held Nola so her head rested on his shoulder. "And so will you. I'm not going to let anyone hurt you."

"But what if your dad's right? What if all the darkness and blood really are chasing me?" The words felt foolish in her mouth, but it didn't erase the fear Captain Ridgeway had left lodged in her chest.

"They are." Jeremy wrapped both arms around her. "My dad was telling the truth. People in the city know your name. Wolves, Vampers, they've all heard the name *Nola Kent*."

"But why? I'm no one. I'm not important at all." She buried her face in Jeremy's chest, the stench of chemicals obscured his familiar scent of fresh earth, and she hated it. Hated the one who had torn his flesh and left him stuck in this hospital room. She wanted to fight all of them. Find the people who knew her name and destroy every last one of them, until there was no one left to hurt Jeremy.

"You are important." He held her even closer, as though he had sensed her urge to run. "You're important to me because I love you. And important to the domes because you're brilliant."

"But why in the city?" Nola whispered. "Nightland is gone. Emanuel and Kieran are gone. There's no one I've ever met left in the city."

"You were important to Nightland." He pressed his cheek to her hair. "You were important enough for there to be a battle over you. And if you were important enough for us to fight over you, then you're important enough to be a target. Yours is the only dome name people know in the city. It's the only name they can shout."

"What do I do?" Nola held onto Jeremy as tightly as she dared.

"You don't do anything. We will figure it out. Together."

CHAPTER ELEVEN

"I'll be back soon." Nola leaned down and brushed her lips against Jeremy's, unable to keep a smile from the corners of her mouth as he tried to pull her in tighter. "I have to go."

She had already been given a whole day to spend in Jeremy's room, more than anyone but Lenora Kent's daughter would have been granted. And, as far as Nola knew, none of the other injured Outer Guard had been allowed to have visitors stay in their rooms at all.

Captain Ridgeway hadn't allowed any of the wounded Outer Guard to be moved to the hospital wing, insisting on keeping his men separate from the injured Dome Guard.

The lines between Dome Guard and Outer Guard had always been thick. Two arms meant to be doing the same thing but hating each other all the while.

The Dome Guard alternated between calling the Outer Guard violent and incompetent, depending on how riots ended. And the Outer Guard called the Dome Guard cowards for never going out into the city.

Then half the Dome Guard had been dragged away to help

stop the fighting. Some had been injured, and four of them killed. But still the line between the two sections seemed as stiff as ever.

"If you don't get out of my way, I'll bring your name before the Council!" The shout pounded through the door from the corridor.

Jeremy moved toward the edge of the bed and was halfway to standing before Nola put both hands on his chest, trying to keep him still.

"You're not supposed to get up," she said as the shouting voice came closer.

"My men fought alongside yours against the wolves, Ridgeway!" Nola recognized Captain Stokes' voice as his words became crisper, as though he were right outside the door. "And if you expect me to allow you to use *my men* to fight in your damned city again, I want answers!"

Before she could wonder at Stokes' foolhardy courage in shouting at Captain Ridgeway while surrounded by a flock of Outer Guard, stomping footsteps approached.

"If you don't mind"—Nola gasped as her mother's voice cut through Captain Stokes' shouts—"I need to get through this door to collect my daughter. Some of us in the domes are still trying to be productive rather than having pissing contests and shouting in the hall like spoiled children."

Nola was already halfway across the room when a sharp knock sounded the instant before the door swung open. "Nola, it's time to work," Lenora said in a dangerous voice that shot tension into Nola's shoulders. "Jeremy, I hope you're feeling better and can get some rest. That is *if* these cretins who call themselves captains can stop shouting like a couple of common city dwellers."

Nola didn't dare look back as she followed her mother out into the hall.

Captain Ridgeway and Captain Stokes stood ten feet apart, glaring daggers at one another.

Nola ran past her mother and up the stairs, not stopping until the next landing.

"I will not have my authority questioned by a man who knows as little about the state of the city as an earthworm!" Captain Ridgeway's voice carried up the steps.

Lenora made a sound somewhere between a *tsk* and a growl as she strode past Nola and down the hall. "How on earth do they expect to gain anyone's respect by shouting?"

Nola was glad her mother had moved in front of her and couldn't see the look of astonishment on her face.

"In troubling times, we have to stand together, not push away others who should be our allies," Lenora said.

"Was there a Council meeting this morning?" Nola jogged to catch up to her mother whose words sounded suspiciously like Council parroting.

"Yes, there was."

Nola didn't need to ask how the meeting had gone.

"So, where am I going to be working today?" she asked, more for something to say that didn't involve the Council meeting or the shouting guards below than because she really wanted to know.

"You'll be working with the outsiders again." Lenora looked at her daughter with a furrowed brow. "Just because our work was interrupted doesn't mean it doesn't have to be finished. I let you have all day yesterday to sit with Jeremy. But the world keeps turning, and quite frankly we have more to do now than ever. Extra mouths to feed and all."

"Extra mouths to feed?" Nola asked as they reached the stairs to the Amber Dome. She grabbed a gardening uniform off the hooks on the wall.

"The domes need extra help, which means more people to feed." Lenora turned to her daughter, watching impatiently as Nola hastily yanked on her jumpsuit. "Honestly, Nola, you really should think things through."

"Sorry," Nola said, not really sure what she had done wrong.

"You'll be back with your group from before. They seem competent. Just make sure they don't hurt the plants or steal anything." Lenora strode up the stairs and straight to the high platform in the center of the dome, a sure sign the conversation had ended.

"Thanks, Mom," Nola muttered before looking around the dome.

They had gotten a lot of work done the day before. The rows of plants that needed to be condensed were already finished. The existing plants moved to the far end to make room for the new crop.

Lenora had been right. They had needed outside hands to help in the process. The amount of work accomplished during Nola's absence would have taken at least a week for the Domers to do on their own.

One group moved through with carts, harvesting all the food ripe enough to be eaten. The food would be taken down to the distribution center and sent out to the families of the domes. That had always been Nola's favorite part of the work. Taking the food they had grown and sending it away to be eaten.

But the group with the carts weren't Nola's people. She had to make nearly a full lap of the dome, passing a group refitting the underground irrigation pipes, a group on ladders to reach the top of the high rod-like towers where the herbs grew, and another pruning back the dead branches on the fruit-bearing trees before she finally found her group working on a seedling tray.

Three hundred tiny containers of soil lay on a long table, ready to receive the new seeds on the brink of sprouting.

T stood by the seed tray, carefully counting out how many they had. Beauford moved down the row, putting one seed into each container. Catlyn followed behind him, covering each seed and giving it the tiniest bit of water.

"Wow," Nola said, her voice coming out awkwardly bright as she tried to sound encouraging. "You've all done a great job!"

"Thanks." Catlyn gave a quick smile while Beauford only spared a moment to glare at Nola before placing another seed. "It's good to see you back. They didn't tell us where you were. I was worried you had been injured in the evacuation."

"No," Nola said as she tied her hair back, wavering on the point of lying.

Don't add lies. There isn't any reason for it.

"A friend of mine was hurt in the fighting in the city," Nola said.

There was a sharp intake of breath from T's direction.

"Is he okay?" Catlyn asked, pulling Nola's attention away from T.

"It was pretty bad, so they let me sit with him," Nola said, moving closer to T, "but he's doing better now."

"It's amazing what you can do with fancy medicine," Beauford said from down the table. "Save you from all sorts of terrible things."

"My friend was very lucky," Nola said. "But he was hurt trying to help people in the city."

T gripped the edge of the table.

"Are you okay?" Nola asked, softly enough not to be overheard by anyone outside their group.

"Fine, ma'am." T let go of the table and counted another set of seeds into her hand.

"Were...Is your family safe? Did they all make it through the riot?" Nola asked, covering T's hand to stop her working.

The girl didn't brush Nola away, but she didn't look at her either. "I don't have any family in the city."

"And we wouldn't know if they had been hurt anyway." Beauford grabbed the seeds from T's other hand. "We haven't been allowed to leave the damned domes to go back to the city.

Everyone we know could be dead, but they'll keep us locked in here to work."

Catlyn hushed him as one of the Dome Guard headed toward their table.

"Is everything all right here, Miss Kent?" the guard asked, narrowing his eyes at Beauford.

"We're fine," Catlyn said. "Things are moving along."

"I didn't ask you," the guard said roughly to Catlyn before turning to Nola. "Is everything all right here, *Miss Kent*?"

"Y-yes," Nola said, taking a deep breath and trying not to let the gruffness of the guard shake her. "I was actually wondering what time the workers were going to be escorted back to the city tonight."

"Transports in and out of the city have been halted," the guard said. "No point in risking guards' safety while the city is eating itself alive."

"But what if they need to go see their families?" Anger crept into Nola's voice. "What if the workers need to get home?"

"They can go whenever they like." The guard glared at Beauford who stood next to Nola, blatantly not working. "Anyone who doesn't want to stay and work for the domes is free to leave. They're used to the outside air, they can walk back to the city."

"We just won't be let back in or paid for our work," Beauford said. "But we're free to go back to the burning city and starve whenever we like."

"Then perhaps you should be grateful for the food and bed we've given you." The guard turned to Nola. "Would you like me to have him removed from your group?"

"No!" she said too loudly.

The guard narrowed his eyes.

"I think we're all just a little stressed from the last few days," Nola said. "Beauford can stay with my team."

The guard nodded. "I'll report him to Dr. Kent. She should be kept informed of workers who cause trouble."

Leaving his threat lingering in the air, the guard turned and strode to the center platform.

"Look busy right now," Nola spoke through gritted teeth, grabbing a few seeds and moving to the closest pots. Even Beauford had the sense to follow her lead.

After a minute or so, she glanced back at the platform. The guard had gone, but Lenora stared in their direction, watching the group work.

Running out of seeds in her hand, Nola moved back to T. "Can I get another handful?"

T passed Nola a little dish of seeds.

"Please be careful with them," T said. "They only gave us enough for the pots. I think they're afraid of us trying to smuggle seeds out. If we ever get out."

Nola worked on the closest tiny seed pot, miming planting since that soil had already been filled. "Do you want to leave?"

"I doubt I'd have any place to go," T said, her voice shockingly calm. "Where I was staying, it was right near Nightland. If the fighting was as bad as it sounds, I can't imagine I'd have a place to go back to. The tunnels are valuable to vampires and wolves. If there was a big fight, it would have been there."

"But the Domers went out to fight—" Nola stopped working as T's eyes widened. "What?" she whispered, moving closer to T, pretending to need more seeds though she hadn't used any. "If the big fight was Domers and wolves, it might not have been near Nightland. The domes don't want anything to do with those tunnels."

"You're right," T said. "Maybe I'm just being pessimistic. I might still have a place to live and a few friends left alive. No way to find out, but I might be that lucky. Or, maybe the world's turned even more inside out. I did just hear a Domer say *Domer* after all."

"What do you mean?" Nola looked back down at the pots,

pretending to plant more seeds, grateful her hands didn't tremble and betray her.

"I've never heard a Domer say *Domer*." T moved in closer, so her shoulder touched Nola's.

"Have you known many people from the domes?" Nola asked, carefully not saying *Domer*.

"No." T shrugged, jarring the dish in Nola's hand. "But I've known even more Vampers than you have, Magnolia Kent. And Vampers say vampires, and Domers say whatever the hell name you like to call yourselves that makes you feel better about the whole world hating you."

"The world doesn't hate us," Nola said.

"Of course, they do," T said, switching Nola's full seed dish out for another full seed dish. "You should know that better than anyone. Emanuel would have made sure of that."

___

CHAPTER TWELVE

___

The air in Nola's lungs froze. There was no way for her to breathe. Nothing for her to do. Fear had consumed her body.

Emanuel would have made sure of that.

The dome spun for a second before everything went black.

"Magnolia," a distant and unfamiliar voice called. "Magnolia, are you all right?"

No! the voice in Nola's head screamed. *Nothing is all right. Nothing has ever been all right!*

But her lips formed other words as her eyes fluttered open. "I'm fine."

She was in the medical wing, on a bed with a bright light overhead.

Doctor Mullins leaned over her, concern wrinkling her brow.

"What happened?" Nola tried to sit up, but the doctor placed a firm hand on her shoulder, pressing her back onto the bed.

"You fainted," Doctor Mullins said. "In the Amber Dome. Do you remember?"

"Yeah." Shame and fear pinked Nola's cheeks. "Yeah, I do."

"Your levels are all fine," Doctor Mullins said. "You want to tell me what happened?"

"I panicked. I was talking to one of the outsiders. They...they mentioned Nightland, and I just panicked." Nola hoped her answer would be close enough to the truth for the doctor to allow her to leave without asking any more questions.

"You weren't feeling faint or nauseous?"

"No." She shook her head. "I just freaked."

"It's okay." Doctor Mullins took her hand from Nola's shoulder, allowing her to sit up. "You've been through a lot, Magnolia. More than most could handle. If you need to talk to someone, we can make arrangements—"

"I really don't want to talk." Nola pushed herself to her feet and swayed as the room began to tilt again.

The doctor grabbed her elbow, steadying her.

"Thank you, but I'm fine. I just want to do my work and help the domes and..." Nola's voice faded away. She didn't know what else she wanted to do.

"I understand." The doctor took Nola's hand. She was young, probably only ten years older than Nola, and there she was, a doctor. Saving people. "I know what it's like to want to help. But you have to take care of yourself, too. If you want to talk, let me know and we'll arrange something."

"Thank you." Nola hurried toward the door.

"And if you start feeling faint or dizzy, sit down and have someone call for help. If the outsiders brought in an illness, we need to find it."

"Is one of them sick?" Nola asked.

"The pregnant one fainted in the Amber Dome yesterday," the doctor said, the tone of concern she had had for Nola all but gone. "I ran some tests and there's nothing we can find, but it's always best to be alert."

"But what about the baby? Did you make sure the baby was all right?"

"There isn't much to be done." The doctor shrugged. "She's an outsider. We can't give her dome medicine. She's already eating dome food. And who knows what damage the child was already subjected to in utero? I have enough patients with the guards who were hurt in the attacks and the dome citizens who need routine medical care. I can't add another patient who isn't even mine to care for." She opened the door for Nola. "No more work for you today. You need to go home and rest, but make sure you get something to eat first."

"Thanks." Nola was out the door and into the hall in a moment, walking as quickly as she dared.

How could a doctor not care about the health of an innocent child?

It's Nightland's fault.

Nightland had made the domes' existence so precarious. Nightland had made the city so violent. The Vampers and the wolves were the ones to blame for the horrible things that were happening. It wasn't the domes' fault that T and her baby might be sick.

It's our fault if we don't do anything to help.

Nola stopped at the end of the hall. She could go to Bright Dome. Eat, then go see Jeremy. Pretend Doctor Mullins had never mentioned T at all.

She turned around and walked back to the room where she had woken up.

"Actually," Nola said as soon as she stepped into the room, making Doctor Mullins jump, "I've been feeling a little run-down, what with—" She gave a weak smile and, just as Gentry had done days ago, waved a hand as though to say *everything*. "Would it be all right if I got a vitamin pack? Just to make sure I don't catch anything."

Doctor Mullins stared at Nola for a moment, her gaze seeming to take in everything from the slight purple under her eyes to her shrinking frame. The Domers were never given pills unless they were ill. Their diets were carefully controlled so they received all the nutrients they needed from food. Vitamin packs were reserved for the ill and endangered.

"I'm glad you're willing to admit you aren't feeling well." Doctor Mullins moved to a locked cabinet in the corner. "Being in tune with your body is the first step toward staying healthy." She pulled down a little glass bottle and handed it to Nola. "Take these with each meal and come back in a week, we'll see if you're feeling more yourself. In the meantime, remember, whether it's anxiety or just dizziness, come and see me."

"Yes, I will. Thank you." Nola backed out of the room. "I appreciate it." As soon as the door shut, she ran down the hall, the feeling of having stolen from the domes chasing her the whole way.

She headed straight for the Amber Dome, keeping the little glass bottle hidden in her palm. Her heart raced. What she was doing was wrong. A terrible offense against the domes.

No worse than what you've already done.

She climbed the steps to the Amber Dome, nodding at the guards who seemed shocked to see her on her feet so soon.

"Nola," Lenora called from the high platform.

To Nola's surprise, Lenora came down from her perch, hurrying toward her daughter.

"Nola, what are you doing here?" Lenora crossed her arms and examined her daughter's face. "The doctor sent word you needed to rest."

"I am." Nola corrected herself. "I'm going to. I just want to make sure my team is okay, and then I'll sleep, I promise."

"I'll see you at home." Lenora climbed back up to her platform.

For a moment, Nola considered telling her mother she wouldn't be at home, but by the time her mother made it back to their little house, she would have forgotten to worry about her daughter anyway.

She walked over to her group, careful not to hurry, though instinct told her to run.

"Miss Kent," Catlyn said as soon as she caught sight of her. "Are you feeling better?"

"Yes, thank you," Nola said, walking straight over to T.

Fear flashed through T's eyes for a moment before she stiffened her jaw as though ready to be struck.

"T," Nola said, stopping so close to the other girl that her face was only a foot away, "the doctor said that you were shaky, that there might be something wrong with your baby."

T's face paled.

"It's not much, and I don't know if it will help, but take one of these with every meal." Nola took T's hand in hers, pretending to lead her the two feet back to the worktable. "It's only a supplement, but it's the best I could get my hands on without people asking questions."

"I—" T began.

"Don't let anyone find out about these, or we'll both be walking into the city." Nola looked to the other two outsiders. "I'm sure you'll be able to finish without me. I'll see you tomorrow."

"Why?" T murmured, not looking away from the table in front of her.

"Because I'm not like Emanuel," Nola said. "I don't like to watch innocent people suffer."

Without giving T a chance to respond, she turned and walked through the dome and down the stairs.

It wasn't until she had made it three corridors away from the Amber Dome that Nola leaned against the wall. Her heart raced. Sweat slicked her palms, and a pounding pain gnawed at the back of her skull.

I've made a terrible mistake.

She had helped an outsider, gone against the domes again. If anyone found out, she would be banished to a city that had turned into a war zone. And she hadn't helped just anyone. She had helped a girl who knew Emanuel. At least well enough to know Nola had spent time with him. Stayed in his home and helped save his daughter's life.

Taking a shuddering breath, she pushed herself off the wall and forced her feet to move. Biting her lips to keep them from trembling, she nodded to the people she passed. Waiting for one of them to run at her screaming she was a traitor.

The guard at the top of the barracks stairs didn't try to stop her but instead gave her a wry smile as she hurried down the steps.

She knocked on Jeremy's door, hoping there wouldn't be anyone in there with him.

"Come in," he called.

Nola wrenched open the door and was inside in an instant, locking the door before running to Jeremy's bedside.

"What's going on?" Concern coated Jeremy's face as he moved to get out of bed.

"Careful." Nola tried to push Jeremy back into bed, but he threw his legs over the side as though she weren't holding him back at all.

"What's wrong?"

"Please be careful," Nola said, finally managing to stop Jeremy before he actually stood up.

"You just ran in here like there was a Vamper on your tail, and you want me to be careful?" Jeremy took her hands in his. "What the hell is going on? Is there something happening aboveground?"

"Yes—no." She searched for the best words to tell Jeremy what she'd done. "I mean, I passed out. I'm okay," she pushed on when his eyes grew wide. "One of the outsiders in my work group. She knows I know Emanuel. And I panicked. That's why I fainted. What if she tells someone I helped Nightland?"

"No one would believe her." Jeremy pressed his hands to Nola's cheeks. He was so tall even sitting down his face was level with hers. "She's one outsider. They'll think she's crazy, they'll think she's working for Emanuel, trying to infiltrate the domes and cause trouble."

"But what if Emanuel *did* send her? What if he wants to make me help them again, and I already did. Jeremy, I did something stupid. Really, really stupid."

"What did you do?"

"The girl, T is what she's called, she's pregnant," Nola said, begging him to understand, knowing she couldn't blame him if he decided this was the last straw and turned her over to the Dome Council himself. "She hasn't been doing very well. And she might be working for Emanuel, but that's got nothing to do with her baby, so I asked for a vitamin pack and gave it to her."

Jeremy let go of Nola's face and buried his head in his hands.

"I'm sorry." She sat on the bed next to Jeremy. "I'm so, so sorry. I just got caught up, and the doctor said she wouldn't help T because she's an outsider. But that baby has never done anything to hurt anyone. And I didn't think, until I did think, and now... I'm so sorry."

"The doctor was right, Nola!" Jeremy half-shouted, just softly enough not to be heard in the hall. "That girl has nothing to do with us. She is an outsider. One who might be working for Emanuel, You said it yourself."

"But the baby—"

"Isn't your problem."

"But it should be." Nola took Jeremy's hands in hers, kneeling on the bed so she could look straight into his eyes. "I'm sorry, I know I've messed up and keep messing up. I know what the domes stand for is important. We are the future. And maybe it makes me broken. Maybe I should just be banished. But I can't work next to a pregnant girl who needs medical help and not even try to do anything. And I know that's wrong," her voice faded. "But I didn't know what else to do. I'm sorry."

Silence filled the room for a moment, tainted only by the faint humming of the air ducts.

"You aren't broken," Jeremy said. "They founded the domes to give future generations of children a fighting chance in the rotting world we've been left with. But it isn't a perfect system. The founders laid out a whole bunch of rules, and I don't think any of them thought we'd want to break them. The outside world wasn't made up of monsters and starving people when the domes were built. The founders didn't know what we'd be watching happen on the other side of the glass. But you can't save them all, Nola. And helping that girl could mean hurting your own people."

"But it's so tiny to us." Tears welled in her eyes. "And what if it saves her baby?"

"But what about when T has to go back outside?" Jeremy wrapped his arms around her, laying his cheek against her hair. "You haven't been out there, not lately. It's gotten worse. Worse than when there was a riot at the food center. I know you were in Nightland. But the city isn't being run by one psychopath who might actually be able to control his people anymore. There are no more jobs. Give it a few more months and there will be no more food. It might be kinder if that baby wasn't born."

"But if they can find a way to farm, then they could eat," she whispered, letting Jeremy hold her close, sure she would shatter into a million irreparable pieces if he let go.

"For a while," he said. "Until others found out they had food and tried to take it from them. Or there was a bad storm. Or a new sickness came."

"So you're saying everyone outside the glass is doomed?" Nola said, the finality of her words striking her in the chest.

"Eventually, yes." He held her tighter, as though he could sense the terrible pain growing inside her, threatening to send her back into blackness. "Humans won't be able to survive outside the domes, not for a long time."

"But what about Vampers and wolves?" Nola asked. "Are they doomed, too?"

"They'll make it the longest," Jeremy said. "They're the strongest, and some run in big enough groups to take what they need to survive."

"Like Nightland." She remembered the Vampers coming through the glass, the blood that slicked the floors of the halls. "And the ones that do survive will pick each other off. And then they'll come for us."

"Then they'll come for us," Jeremy said. "That girl's baby might survive. But if it lives long enough, it'll end up our enemy."

"But it isn't now." Nola looked into his eyes. "And if we decide someone is our enemy before they can decide themselves, aren't we losing the chance of there ever being peace?"

"I love you, Nola." He leaned down and kissed her. "I love you for always wanting to see the good. But the world has fallen too far. All that's left is survival. It's my job to keep you safe, and I can't let you risk yourself for a girl who might be working for Emanuel."

She wanted to argue. To say that there was still good in the world, and maybe there could be peace between the domes and the outside.

But Jeremy was right. The gap between the desperate and the privileged was too great. The domes had to stay intact to ensure the survival of the human race, and the outside couldn't be saved from burning. If that had been possible, the domes would never have been built in the first place.

"What do I do?" Nola said. "Just wait and see if she says anything else? Let her keep spying for Emanuel if that's what she's here to do? Wait and see if she turns me in?"

"Nola, calm down," Jeremy hushed as her voice rose in panic. "You're going to talk to this girl and see what she knows."

"How? I can't just ask if she's going to turn me in for helping Nightland in the middle of the Amber Dome."

"We'll wait till they're back in the bins tonight," Jeremy said, lying back on the bed and drawing her down with him so her head rested on his shoulder. "I know where they're being kept, and I can get you in. Then we just ask her a few questions."

"And if she is going to tell the Council something that will get me sent away?"

"We convince her to keep her mouth shut."

CHAPTER THIRTEEN

Hours passed with Nola lying in Jeremy's arms. He drifted in and out of sleep, but all she could do was stare up at the ceiling and wait. A guard had brought a tray in for Jeremy a few hours ago. She had the feeling that if Jeremy hadn't been the captain's son, they might not have been so kind about her and Jeremy being alone in his room. As it was, she only had to endure a few obnoxious winks from the food bearer before they were left alone.

The lights had dimmed, and people had stopped passing in the hallway when Jeremy finally kicked off his sheets.

"You should stay here," Nola said one more time though she knew it was useless. "You have to be careful."

"I'm a fast healer." Jeremy laced his fingers through hers as he led her to the door. "And if that girl is working for Emanuel, I'm not letting you anywhere near her without me."

"Jeremy." She stepped in front of him, blocking his path to the door at the last moment. "I love you. And I'm sorry for getting you involved in any of this."

He leaned down and kissed her, wrapping his arms around her, and lifting her so her toes barely touched the ground. She draped her arms around his neck, twining her fingers through his short hair to pull him even closer. The pounding of his heart echoed in her chest, making her own heart race quicker.

She gasped as he pulled away.

"I never thought loving you would be easy." Jeremy pressed his lips to the top of her head. "You don't get something as wonderful as you without having to work for it. And I'm willing to do whatever it takes."

"You're better than I could ever deserve, Jeremy Ridgeway."

"I'll let you keep believing that." He smiled and opened the door.

The dim night setting of the lights cast shadows in the corridor. Two guards stood by the stairs, their backs to the barracks. Jeremy walked calmly toward the door at the end of the hall.

Nola felt like they should run. Or try to hide in the faint shadows that hovered near the walls. But Jeremy walked boldly and silently forward, not hesitating or looking back as he pulled open the door that led to the row of locked rooms.

Letting the door swing quietly shut behind them, Jeremy turned to Nola. "I don't know what the girl looks like."

"What if one of the guards saw us come in here?" she whispered. "If they catch us in here, you could get in trouble. What if they kick you out, too? I never should have let you get out of bed, let alone help me."

Jeremy stepped in and silenced her with a kiss. "I'm going to help you. And if anyone finds us in here?" He shrugged. "It won't be the best, but I wouldn't be the first Outer Guard to have snuck a girl into this hall. No one's supposed to talk about the bins, so it's a dark corner where people won't come looking."

"I had never heard of them." Nola blushed, trying not to think of what Jeremy's father or her mother would say if they were caught in the middle of the night in a forbidden hallway lined with private rooms she shouldn't even know about in the first place.

"Don't let T see you," Nola said, leading Jeremy to the window where she had seen T before. "If she is going to tell the Council about me, I don't want her to know about you, too."

T wasn't in the room she had been in last time. That one had been taken over by men. She moved to the next window, careful to stop Jeremy just out of sight. But T wasn't in that room or the next. Apparently, the guards didn't care about returning the outsiders to the same rooms every night.

She peeked into the second-to-last window. T was there, lying on a bunk, her head in Catlyn's lap. Nola dodged out of sight of the window, her heart racing.

"The fighting." Nola clung to Jeremy's hand. "When you fought the wolves in the city, where were you fighting?"

"It started on the old Vamper row"—Jeremy's face paled—"by Nightland. The strip of falling-down houses leading up to it. But we got penned in by two different packs who wanted to kill each other and didn't hate the idea of killing a bunch of guards in the process. We had to fight all the way back to the bridge."

Nola rose up on her toes, kissing Jeremy before whispering, "I'm so glad you made it home." She let her cheek rest on his for a moment before pushing him back into the shadows.

Taking a deep breath, she tapped on the window.

Catlyn leapt to her feet, looking ready for a fight. When she saw Nola's face in the shadows, her brows pinched together.

"I want to see T," Nola said.

Catlyn cocked her head to the side and moved closer, apparently unable to hear.

Nola glanced at the door that led to the barracks, and then at Jeremy before saying more loudly, "I need to talk to T."

Catlyn heard that time, as did the rest of the women in the room, all of whom now stared at Nola.

"T," Nola said, jumping right in before the girl had even reached the door. "How did you know I've met Emanuel?"

Fear passed through T's eyes before she spoke.

"Everyone in the city knows you were in Nightland." T raised her chin defiantly. "You're the reason Nightland attacked the domes. In retribution—"

"That's a lie, and you know it," Nola said. "Nightland attacked us because they are thieving, murdering cowards who wanted what the domes have."

Jeremy tightened his grip on Nola's hand.

"Now tell me, how did you know I've met Emanuel?"

T studied her for a moment before answering. When she spoke she said each word carefully, as though measuring every impact. "I was in Nightland. My baby's father is a vampire of Nightland. He told me about the Domer who had helped Emanuel's little girl. I saw you there, dancing with the Doctor's son, Kieran Wynne."

Nola swayed, but Jeremy didn't let go of her hand.

"So you saw me there," Nola said. "So what? Why would you think Emanuel would have taught me anything?"

"Because he must have." T leaned in toward the window so her breath fogged the glass. "You were there, you know Kieran, you stayed in Emanuel's home. I heard the order shouted by Kieran himself that you weren't to be touched. He loved you. You're helping them."

"No, I'm not!" Nola's voice echoed down the hall. She froze, staring at the door to the Outer Guard barracks, waiting for guards to come running in. A full minute passed before she looked back at T. "I thought I knew Emanuel and Kieran. But they lied to me. They betrayed me."

"But you have to know," T said, her eyes boring into Nola's as though hoping to rip information straight from her mind. "You have to know where Nightland went."

"What?" The absurdity of it forced a laugh into Nola's throat. "Know where they went? Is that really what you're after? I didn't know they were going to attack or leave. They lied to me. They used me. Do you really think they would have told me where they were going? If I knew, the guards would already have destroyed them."

"But Emanuel and Kieran—"

"Used me," Nola said, disgust replacing all fear. "They're monsters just like the rest of Nightland."

"You really don't know where they are?" T's face crumpled, and for the first time she looked like the nineteen-year-old she was. "There really isn't a way to find them?"

"Why would you want to?" Nola said. "Why would you want to find a bunch of murderers?"

"They weren't all like that," T said. "Some of them were good. Charles was good. He never would have hurt anyone."

"Charles is the baby's father?" Nola asked, not needing T's nod to know she was right. "Was he with Nightland when they attacked us?"

"I don't know," T said. "He told me to stay inside. He left me with food and told me to lock the door behind him. By the time I came out, the domes were shattered, and Nightland was empty. But if I can find Emanuel and the vampires, they might know where he is."

Nola's anger splintered.

She's alone and pregnant.

"I'm sorry," Nola said.

"I'm not going to be able to find him, am I?" T said.

Catlyn came up from behind and wrapped an arm around T.

"We'll make it through just like we always have," Catlyn said.

"You need to stay here for as long as the domes will let you." Nola hated to pile more terribleness on top of everything else. "You were right. The fighting in the city a few nights ago, it was near the entrance to Nightland. I don't think you can go home."

Tears streamed down T's face. "Now he won't be able to find me even if he does come back. It really is over."

"I'm sorry," Nola said again. She began to say *If there's anything*

I can do but stopped herself. There was nothing she could do. The domes would never allow it.

"Thank you," T said.

Nola nodded, not trusting herself to speak.

"And don't worry." T pressed her hand to the small window that separated them. "I won't tell the guards anything. I guess we both fell in love with a vampire who abandoned us."

Nola felt Jeremy tense beside her but didn't dare look away.

"We both survived the vampires," Nola said, "and Nightland. We just have to keep on surviving."

"Thank you," Catlyn said, taking T by the elbow and leading her away.

Nola stepped away from the window and buried her face in Jeremy's chest. She wished he hadn't been standing there. Hadn't heard what T had said.

"I'm sorry," Nola whispered, so quietly no one on the other side of the door would be able to hear.

"Don't be." Jeremy held her tightly. "You were right, about you both being survivors. Nightland hurt both of you. The way that bastard manipulated you—"

"Don't. Please don't. I don't want to think about that ever again. It makes me feel sick and filthy, and I hate it."

Jeremy kissed the top of her head before tipping her chin up so he could look into her eyes. "I will never, ever let any of them touch you again. I swear to you, Nola. I'll keep you safe."

"I know." She leaned up and kissed him, letting anger and fear flake away at the taste of his lips. "I believe you. But T. What is she going to do?"

"The Vamper should have thought about that before he got a girl pregnant and abandoned her in the city." Jeremy's mouth twisted in disgust. "The domes' rules might be harsh sometimes, but at least we don't have a bunch of fatherless babies starving. And even if there weren't rules, I would never leave you like that." Jeremy's face turned pink as he looked down at Nola. "What I mean is—I mean I wouldn't..." Jeremy mouthed wordlessly for a moment.

Nola pressed her hand to her mouth to dampen her feeble laugh as his face turned from pink to scarlet.

Giving up on words and shaking his head instead, he led her back down the hall.

Pushing the door to the barracks corridor open a crack, he peered through before leading Nola out into the hall.

One of the guards at the stairs turned to look at them, smirking at Nola and winking at Jeremy before turning back around. It was Nola's turn to blush as Jeremy led her back into his room.

"At least we know you're safe. I wish we could have talked to her away from the others," Jeremy said, lowering himself onto the bed. Nola took his arm, trying to help him, but instead, he pulled her to lay next to him.

"I think T and Catlyn will keep them from talking." Nola untied the knot at the end of her hair, shaking her curls free of the tight braid. "If the domes knew T had ties that close to Night-land, they never would have let her in." *Ties that close* seemed an insufficient term for *carrying a Vamper's baby*. "That'll have to be enough for tonight."

She lay down on the bed, letting herself melt into Jeremy's shoulder.

"No matter what T says," Jeremy said, his voice growing fainter with each word, "we're in this together. I won't let them take you from me."

In a minute, Jeremy's breathing was steady and even. But Nola couldn't sleep. What if she had been the one with a child growing inside of her? Abandoned by Kieran, not knowing where he had gone?

She held tightly to the front of Jeremy's shirt, promising herself that he wouldn't run from her.

The outsiders didn't have the same marriage laws the domes

lived by. There were no children born without fathers in the domes. In order to gain permission to have a child in the domes, you had to apply to the Council and go through genetic testing to ensure healthy offspring. She knew some people had snuck into the far corners of the glass, or met in dark passages, in the middle of the night. But unapproved children couldn't be allowed. The domes' population had to be methodically controlled. Even with the loss of life in the attacks, they still would have to be careful to repopulate according to dome needs.

But in the outside world, there was no Council to say who was allowed to be the father of your child. Only a young girl in love with a vampire. And now she was locked in a cell, with no hope for a safe place for her child to be born.

Tears burned in the corners of Nola's eyes as she fell asleep. A faint shadow haunted her dreams. A boy she loved, staring down at her as she held their child in her arms.

CHAPTER FOURTEEN

Dazzling blue filled the bright sky. The gray smoke had stopped drifting up from the domes. The last of the bodies had been burned, and as Nola looked out over the hill there was no sign that anything terrible had ever happened to the domes. The glass that had been shattered in the attack had been repaired or replaced. Cleaning the ventilation systems and making the glass stronger than it had been before were the only things the outsiders were still working on in the atrium and the Grassland Dome. But the labor in the Amber Dome was far from finished.

It had been three days since she and Jeremy had visited T in the locked rooms. Three days of nothing. No alarms, no scares. Waking up, working, seeing Jeremy, sleeping. It amazed Nola that three days could now feel like a new normal. After everything that had happened, three days of calm seemed an incredible gift. Jeremy had moved into the large barracks room and would begin duty again soon. Nola had gone back to sleeping in her own room. Peace had settled over the domes.

She didn't even know she had been humming until T poked her in the arm. "Nola. What's going on?"

T had given up on calling Nola *Miss* after their evening meeting. Their brief talk through the glass had forged a tenuous camaraderie between them.

Nola smiled as T cocked her head, examining her.

"Nothing." Nola grinned. "Just having a good morning."

"Well, then." T smiled back before moving down the long line of new seed trays that were their day's work.

Nola reveled in the feeling of the warm earth under her fingers. Planting a seed, knowing it would grow into food that would provide for the domes.

"It's a little strange," Catlyn said from down the row, "that your botanist mother named you after a flower, isn't it?"

"What?" Nola laughed.

"Well, it's a bit strange, don't you think?" Catlyn said.

"Leave it, Catlyn," Beauford said.

"My mother likes plants, so she named me after a flower. Is that weird?" Nola asked.

The guards turned to look over at them. Nola skipped a few pots, moving closer to the others so she could speak more quietly. "I mean, how do they choose names on the outside?"

"The same as anyone chooses a name," Beauford said. "Pick a name, call a kid it, and be done." He stalked back to the front of the row and took an overly long time grabbing seeds.

"I still don't understand why my name is strange," Nola said.

"It's not your name she's worried about," T said. "Catlyn is unhappy with how I want to name *my* baby."

"Naming it after a man who abandoned you," Catlyn said. "Tell her, Miss Kent, tell her that's an awful idea."

Nola froze for a moment as both women stared at her. "Do you know if it's a boy?" she asked, hoping to dodge the name question.

"Charlie could be either a boy's or a girl's name," T said. "Don't you think it's nice, Nola?"

"It's great," Nola said. "If that's what you want."

"A constant reminder of a man who ran out on you?" Catlyn's voice dripped with disgust.

"He didn't run out. It's more complicated than that, and you know it," T said.

Nightland. They were going to talk about Nightland. They were moving from planting seeds and worrying about baby names to Nightland.

Shadows shouldn't be allowed to destroy sunny mornings.

"How did you get your name, T?" Nola asked.

"I don't know." T shrugged. "It's not my real name. At least not all of it. I think it was a nickname, or a shortening of my name. But my parents died when I was little, and the lady that took me in kept calling me T. She died too, though. By the time I thought to ask what T was short for, everyone who would have known was gone. So, I stuck with T."

It felt like someone had punched a hole straight through Nola's stomach. T carried on, working as though she hadn't said anything strange or sad at all. Like having no one alive who could tell you your real name was an ordinary thing.

"And as for you, Catlyn"—T turned back to her, pointing with a dirt-covered finger—"I'm the one carrying the baby, and I'll name it whatever I damn well please. Maybe I'll make it a tradition and call the baby C."

Catlyn *tsked* and flicked T's hand away.

"We should hurry," Nola said, grateful for once for the presence of the ever-watchful guards. Glad to have the excuse to walk away and work on the other side of the tray. A normal day. That was what she craved. A day filled with happiness, untainted by fear. A schedule she knew how to follow, and a task to call her own. She hadn't been able to start back in classes yet. No one had even mentioned when she would be allowed to return to school.

She felt selfish and angry. She was well-fed and had a bed to sleep in.

I want my life back.

A low chime sounded overhead.

At once, all the Domers stopped, calmly waiting for what would come next. The outsiders glanced around fearfully.

Nola ran over to Catlyn and T, who stood frozen as the chime sounded again.

"It's okay," Nola said. "It's just an announcement. It isn't like the sirens."

A voice had already begun to speak.

"Citizens of the domes. In light of the recent tragedies that have been inflicted upon these domes by the troubles in the city, the Council has requested replacement citizens be brought to live in our community. The twenty-five new residents will be transferring from their home domes tonight. While the majority of new residents are going to be moving directly into the Guard barracks, there will need to be a few adjustments to housing. Any domes' citizen whose housing arrangements will be required to change will be notified immediately. We appreciate your cooperation and understanding and hope you will welcome your new neighbors with open arms. They have left their homes to help us in protecting ours."

With a faint *crackle*, the speakers went silent.

More people were coming to join the domes. Twenty-five people none of them had ever met were leaving their own far away domes to come and share Nola's home.

"If they wanted more people to fight for the domes, you think they would have looked to those starving in the city," Beauford said loudly enough for the guards fifty feet away to hear.

Catlyn and T both turned away from him as though wanting to distance themselves from his words. Though it stung, Nola knew he was right. They had workers living in cells in the domes. It would have been kinder to give them a permanent home instead of bringing in others, but it would never have been allowed.

They aren't like us.

They were outsiders. They hadn't been given a dome education and had spent too long in the filthy air, drinking polluted water, and eating the contaminated food to be approved for breeding.

Beauford wasn't the only outsider who seemed unhappy about the announcement. A woman on the other side of the Amber Dome screeched at the Domer in charge of her group.

"You're going to throw us out to starve? You've got extra food and space and you're going to send us out into the city as soon as you're done with us? Let us burn in the riots or bleed for the vampires? Better yet, be meat to feed the wolves? You're worse monsters than any of them! At least when a wolf wants you dead, he's got the courtesy to do it fast with no lies about saving the world or pretending it isn't plain old murder!"

A sharp *pop* sounded from the pack of guards. A tiny silver dart hit the side of the woman's neck, dropping her to the ground.

The dart only contained a sedative to make the woman sleep, but the outsiders didn't seem to know or care.

The others in the screaming woman's group ran forward, stepping between her and the guard that had shot the woman. Shouts echoed from all sides of the Amber Dome as people started to panic.

"They're going to kill us!" A man charged toward the guards, hitting one in the stomach with a shovel before being knocked backward by another guard, who shot a silver dart into his neck.

All of the guards in the dome surged toward the fighting. And the rest of the outsiders ran toward the fight as well.

"Beauford, no!" Catlyn screamed, catching his arm as he moved to join the fray.

A young man had run forward and grabbed a ladder to push back the guards. A dart struck him in the chest, but two women grabbed the ladder, using it like a battering ram to attack the guards.

"It won't help!" T held onto Beauford's other arm, but he was strong. The two women wouldn't be able to hold him much longer.

"Follow me." Nola added her weight to Beauford's arm as she helped Catlyn and T drag him away.

"We can't let them do this to us!" Beauford fought to pull away from them.

"You can't stop it either!" Nola said. "Try and fight if you want, but it'll only be one more dart they have to fire."

Beauford froze for a moment before his arms sagged.

"Good, now come on." Running away from the fighting, Nola led them toward the back of the dome, where thick rows of vines sat low along the wall.

Ducking under the leaves, Nola winced as she felt a vine snap.

More shouting voices filled the dome. Nola glanced back. She could barely make out a dozen black-clad guards running up the stairs to join the fight.

"Get down and be quiet." Nola pushed aside the last of the vines. A set of low, thorny bushes blocked them from the glass. Creating a gap between bushes, she ignored the thorns that pulled at her palms, crouching down and using her weight to case the way through the brambles for the others.

"Are we just going to hide back here?" Beauford said as soon as he was through.

"Yes, we are." Nola leaned back against the glass.

The sounds of the fighting had already changed.

Guards bellowed orders, and Lenora Kent's voice cut above it all.

"I don't care what you're trying to do, stay the hell off my plants!"

Nola smiled. Of course her mother would be standing in the middle of a fight, screaming about plants.

Blood oozed out of the scratches on her hands. She wiped it onto her gardening suit. She would be able to wash her hands soon enough.

"I didn't take you as the type to run from a fight," T whispered as the last of the screaming stopped. "I figured you for the sort to run in and try to stop it."

"That lady shouldn't have attacked the Domer." Nola closed her eyes against the bright sun. "But the domes shouldn't be using you the way they are. Sometimes I feel like the right thing is too abstract for me to understand."

"How poetic," Catlyn said.

"But I do know that all those people will be put outside on the road before dark, and I don't want that to happen to the three of you. The most right thing I could think of was to keep you three safe. So that's what I did."

"Who the hell's got time for a moral compass when north keeps changing?" T said.

"Nola!" A voice shouted from the center of the dome. "Nola!"

"Back here!" Nola called. "Jeremy, we're back here!" Before she could stand, Jeremy had appeared, leaping over plants and dodging through vines to get to her.

"Nola, are you hurt?" Jeremy took her face in his hands.

"I'm fine." She smiled, her heart flipping at the depth of Jeremy's concern for her. "Really, we all are. The fight started, and we ran."

Jeremy kissed her. "Thank you. Thank you for not trying to stop the whole thing yourself."

T and Catlyn grinned behind him.

"And thank you for taking care of her," Jeremy said to the three outsiders. "Come on, let's get you out in the open before they think you got into the tunnels."

"Did outsiders get into the tunnels?" Nola followed Jeremy to the center of the dome.

"Some of them tried," Jeremy said.

The outsiders who had been fighting were all laid out on the ground. Some of them were bloody or had swollen faces. Others looked like they might have been sleeping.

"Nola." Lenora ran up to her daughter. "I should have known that of all the people trusted to work with the outsiders, you would be the only one able to manage them."

"I didn't manage them," Nola said. "They didn't want to fight."

Lenora wasn't listening. "Now we'll have more repair work on top of everything else and no one to help. I think we've proven this is a failed experiment."

"It's not failed," Nola said as two guards stepped toward T, Catlyn, and Beauford. "My group didn't do anything wrong. They're good workers who didn't fight at all."

The two guards walked straight past Nola.

"You three have to come with us," a young female guard said, holding her gun at her side.

"Where are you taking them?" Nola wove through the guards to stand between them and her group.

The guard didn't answer.

"Mom, where are they taking them?" she asked again, her voice rising so Lenora couldn't pretend not to hear. "They didn't do anything wrong. They're good workers, and we need them. Where are you taking my group?"

"Having workers from the outside isn't—"

"Yes, it is!" Nola shouted. Heads turned toward her, but she didn't flinch. "It is for these three. Tell me you aren't going to put them out with the ones who fought. Tell me you're taking them back to the cells you call their rooms and feeding them while we clean up in here."

"Magnolia," Lenora said.

"Mom, tell me you're going to do the right thing." Nola balled her hands into fists, her pulse racing so fast warm blood dripped from her cuts.

"Fine," Lenora said after a long moment. "You've managed well enough with them. But let it be known that if there is one toe stuck out of line, they'll be outside in a minute." Giving the group behind Nola a scathing look, Lenora stalked away.

"If you'll follow us then," the female guard said, her gun still in her hand.

"You can put that away," Nola said.

"You don't have the authority to tell me to do anything." The guard glared coolly at Nola.

"Jeremy, will you walk down with them?" she asked.

"Of course." Jeremy didn't look at Nola or question her as he led the group out of the domes.

Other Dome Guard surrounded the group of downed outsiders. Two guards taking each one and carrying them away. Those who had fought against the domes would wake up on the road outside with no choice but to walk the bridge back to the city and hope they found their homes still standing.

If they even make it that far.

Nola shuddered as two guards lifted the woman who had started the fight, grateful the glass between herself and the outside world was solid once again.

CHAPTER FIFTEEN

The heat of the shower stung the skin on Nola's shoulders, but she didn't turn the temperature down. She knew she should hate herself for standing in hot water, washing with fresh-scented soap while the workers who had fought against the guards trudged toward the city. Toward the dark and unknown.

She took a deep breath, letting the steam fill her lungs.

It's their own fault they were sent away.

That doesn't make marching into the darkness less frightening.

She shut off the water. The urge to run filled her again. To find a way outside the glass and just keep running until there was nothing left to run from.

But there was nowhere to run to. There was nothing to run to. She stepped onto the tiny landing that joined her and her mother's bedroom to the bathroom.

"Nola," Jeremy said.

Nola squeaked and jumped back, banging her shoulder on the doorjamb.

"Sorry." Jeremy stepped out of the shadows at the bottom of the stairs. "I didn't mean to scare you."

Gripping her towel tighter, she turned on the light. "It's fine."

Her heart thundered in her chest as Jeremy dashed up the steps and reached for her hand.

"I just needed to see you, and I thought I would wait down here." Jeremy blushed.

"It's okay." She took his hand, leading him into her room and closing the door behind them. "Is my mom here?"

"No." Jeremy sat down on the bed, holding his head in his hands. "At least I didn't see her."

"What's wrong?" she asked, sitting close enough to Jeremy that her arm pressed into his.

"Gentry's leaving." He didn't look at Nola as he spoke. "She might already be gone."

"Leaving? What do you mean leaving? Gentry loves the domes. She's an Outer Guard, she'd never abandon her home."

"She requested a transfer to another set of domes and got approved," Jeremy said. "They're taking her away on the transport that brought the new guards in."

"But why? How?" Nola knelt on the floor in front of him, moving his hands away from his face. "If we needed more people to be brought into the domes here, why would they let her leave?"

"It's"—Jeremy paused, his brow wrinkled as though the thought of it caused him physical pain—"complicated."

"How?"

He pulled Nola up to sit on his lap, resting his head on her bare shoulder.

"Guard stuff," Jeremy said. "With the city and the fighting... she wants out."

"I'm sorry." She pressed her lips to his temple.

"It's not your fault. It isn't anybody's fault. I just, I never thought she'd actually leave."

Nola wrapped her arms around Jeremy, holding him close.

"I mean, I know people have asked to transfer out before," he said, "but I never thought it would be someone I knew. She's leaving for the other side of the world, and I don't know if she'll ever come back. I may never see my sister again."

Nola opened her mouth to say that of course he would see Gentry again, but she couldn't bring herself to lie, even if it might make Jeremy feel better.

There was hardly any transportation between domes. Her mother, who went to conferences once a year, traveled more than anyone else she knew. Transfers were always for things like specialized training. A temporary assignment that lasted a few years. The far south domes had had too many females a few years back, and the spares had been dispersed to other domes. But leaving just because you wanted to, that wasn't a thing people were allowed to do. If Gentry left, there might never be a way for her to come home.

"Dad's a mess." Jeremy's voice was thick with unshed tears. "She had told him she was going to ask the Council for a transfer, but I don't think he thought she would actually go through with it."

"He'll be okay." Nola pressed her cheek to Jeremy's, too afraid to look him in the eye.

She didn't know if Captain Ridgeway would be okay. She didn't know if any of them would be.

"Your dad is tough," Nola pressed on, relieved her voice sounded strong. "You both are. Gentry is a great guard, and she'll be great wherever she ends up."

"You said you wanted to leave," Jeremy said. "Before the domes were attacked, you said you wanted to leave the domes and live on the outside to help people."

"I did." Nola tensed.

Kieran had shown her ways she could be helpful to the people fighting to survive on the outside. It had all seemed worth it. To be out there doing something that mattered. Risking her life to save others had seemed more meaningful than living trapped behind glass, watching the world crumble.

"I would have gone with you." Jeremy twined his fingers through hers. "I would have left everything behind for you."

"I know."

"I would have gone to protect the girl I love, but Gentry's just gone. Do you think she would have forgiven me if I had left?" Jeremy turned to look into Nola's eyes, searching for an honest answer.

"I don't think so." She swallowed the knot in her throat. "I don't think anyone would have forgiven either of us."

"Then how am I supposed to forgive her?"

"I don't know," Nola said. "I don't know if you can, but if she just couldn't take the fighting anymore—"

"It doesn't matter what she could or couldn't take. She shouldn't have left."

She tried to think of something comforting to say that would prove Gentry had been right to leave. But she was abandoning her family and the domes in their time of need.

There is no excuse.

Nola curled up on the bed and pulled Jeremy to lie down next to her.

"You're so beautiful," he whispered, pushing Nola's hair away from her face.

"When I look like a drowned rat?"

"Always." He pulled her closer. Her towel twisted, baring her hip. She reached down to cover herself, but Jeremy was already kissing her.

He smelled like himself again. Like fresh earth, and new life.

"Nola," Jeremy breathed as she pressed herself to him, feeling every curve of his body against hers.

Beep, beep. Beep, beep.

Nola bolted up in bed at the sound, knocking Jeremy to the floor.

"What's that?" Jeremy said, at the same moment Nola asked, "Are you all right?"

Beep, beep. Beep, beep.

PAM *beeped* at her from the wall, flashing a faint blue light. Jeremy scrambled out of sight as Nola pressed the blue light and the screen blinked to life.

Captain Ridgeway's face stared back at her.

"Captain Ridgeway." Nola straightened her towel, blushing to the roots of her dark hair. Her eyes flicked over to Jeremy, who hid pressed into the corner of the wall.

Eyes wide, he put a finger to his lips.

"Captain Ridgeway, is everything okay?" Nola said.

"I'm sorry to disturb you this late at night, Nola." Captain Ridgeway clenched his jaw as he spoke, as though trying not to shout. "But I need you to come to my office as soon as possible."

"Your office?" Nola's voice squeaked. "Why do you need me to come down there?"

He's found out. He's found out you helped Nightland, and now he's going to throw you in the cell right next to Raina's.

"I'll explain as soon as you get here. Do not accept any further communication. Do not let anyone stop you on your way down. Come straight here. Immediately."

"Okay." Nola nodded. "I'll be there in ten minutes."

"Be here in five," the captain said. "And Nola, wear boots and a coat."

The screen went dark.

"Boots and a coat?" Jeremy craned his neck to stare up at the place where his father's face had just been. "He wants you to go outside?"

Before she could think of an answer, the blue light began to flash again.

Beep, beep. Beep, beep.

Nola reached instinctively forward to press the light before stopping herself. "Why would someone else be calling?"

"No idea, but we need to go." Jeremy turned and faced the closed door of Nola's room.

Beep, beep. Beep, beep.

Nola's hands shook as she yanked clean clothes out of her drawers. "What if your dad found out about Nightland? What if he found out you helped me talk to T?"

"He didn't," Jeremy said. "If he knew about that, there would be guards banging on the door to haul you out for banishment."

"That shouldn't feel comforting." She buttoned her pants and yanked on a shirt. "Why does that feel comforting?"

The beeping that had stopped for a moment, resumed.

Jamming on her boots and grabbing her coat, Nola took Jeremy's hand. "You'll come down with me, right?"

"Of course." Jeremy ran with Nola out of the empty house and onto the stone path.

Night had fallen. Only the faint lights coming from the houses lit their way. Overhead, dim reflections sparkled in the glass. Faraway stars, fighting to be seen through the smog and the light of the domes that surrounded them.

Near the stairs to the tunnel, a stronger light came into view. Not the nearby light of the atrium, something much farther away.

A cluster of tiny lights that seemed to be in the wrong place.

"What is that?" Nola pulled Jeremy off the path and toward the glass. Hundreds of lights flickered on the far bank of the river between the domes and the city.

"The bridge," Jeremy said. "It's all by the bridge."

Without waiting for her to stop looking through the glass, Jeremy dragged her at a sprint toward the stairs.

"Why are there people by the bridge?" she panted, running as fast as she could, struggling to keep up with Jeremy's much longer strides.

She had been on the bridge at night twice before. There had been nothing there but wolves and Vampers searching for victims.

A faint *hum* sounded, and Jeremy looked down at the black band on his wrist. "Shit."

"What is it?" Nola asked.

"They want me in uniform." Jeremy pulled Nola to run faster.

Around the next corner, a line of men waited.

Captain Stokes stood in the middle of the hall, blocking the steps to the Outer Guard barracks.

"Miss Kent." Stokes stepped out of line, planting himself in the center of the corridor.

"We have to get downstairs," she wheezed, moving to go around Stokes, but the guards behind him closed ranks.

"I've been called down to the barracks," Jeremy said, danger sounding in his voice.

"You can go down if you like." Stokes gave a hateful little bow. "Miss Kent is coming with me."

"I can't come with you," Nola said, forcing her voice to stay level though her heart still raced. "I have to go to Captain Ridgeway's office. There's something going on by the bridge. He might not have much time to talk to me if he has to go out there."

"That is exactly why you are coming with me." Stokes stepped forward, his guards matching his movement. "We are going up to the Com Room right now."

"Get out of our way," Jeremy said. "Come on, Nola." Leading her by the arm, Jeremy took a step forward.

Stokes stepped right in front of Jeremy. Had Stokes been as tall, they would have been nose-to-nose.

"You think your blood gives you the right to order me around?" Stokes spoke softly. "I will have you out of the domes so fast your father won't even know how he suddenly lost *both* his children."

"You son of a bitch," Jeremy snarled, dropping Nola's arm and punching Stokes hard in the face.

The line of guards descended on him as he hit Stokes in the stomach, leaving the captain sprawled on the floor.

"Nola, run!" Jeremy punched one of the other guards.

Nola froze. She couldn't leave Jeremy fighting one against five. But what help could she be against trained guards?

"Nola, go!" Jeremy kicked another guard in the stomach, sending him flying into the man behind him.

Running as fast as she could, Nola tore down the flight of stairs to the Outer Guard barracks. People sprinted through the corridor, not with the sense of panic that had filled the domes when guards were bloody and wounded, but with practiced urgency.

None of them even seemed to notice her standing at the foot of the stairs, trying to see a way through the pattern.

"Jeremy Ridgeway needs help!" Nola shouted. "Captain Stokes and his men tried to stop us, and now they're fighting him!"

"Carter, Wright, with me," a guard barked to two others before charging up the stairs.

"You should take more!" Nola called after them, but they were already out of sight.

Forcing her way through the corridor, she managed to get to Captain Ridgeway's office. The door swung open the instant she knocked.

"Inside." Captain Ridgeway gabbed Nola's wrist and yanked her into the office, snapping the door shut behind him.

"What's going on?" she asked. Even with the movement of the hall no longer visible, she could still feel the frenetic energy in the air. "We saw lights by the bridge on the way down."

"We?" Captain Ridgeway asked, his eyes boring holes into her.

"I was with Jeremy when you called," Nola said as he pointed for her to sit. "He was coming down here with me. But Stokes got in the way, and Jeremy punched him."

Captain Ridgeway swore under his breath.

"Some Outer Guard went up to help him."

"We can't worry about Jeremy. There isn't time. Something is happening in the city right now, and we cannot allow it to continue."

"What?" Sweat beaded on her palms as Captain Ridgeway pressed on.

"There is a group amassing by the bridge, more than a thousand people. If that many decided to attack the domes—"

"It would be worse than Nightland." Nola's head spun.

Blood-slicked floor. Shattered glass. Bodies to be burned.

"We don't know if they are planning to attack," the captain said. "So far, they've only given us one demand. They want to speak to Nola Kent."

CHAPTER SIXTEEN

Nola grabbed the edge of her seat as the room tilted. "Who? Who wants to talk to me?"

"We don't know." Captain Ridgeway leaned over her. He was so much taller than she was. A tower of strength larger than she could ever grow to be.

"Emanuel." Nola mouthed the word. There wasn't enough air in her lungs to speak.

"I don't think so." Captain Ridgeway crouched down, speaking to her on eye level as though she were a frightened child. "There is absolutely nothing to indicate Emanuel or any trace of Nightland has come back to the city. What we do know is that if the people out there try to cross the bridge, there will be a bloodbath. We have to stop them from crossing that bridge."

She nodded.

"We need you to go out there and talk to them. They've refused to speak to any of my guards. You have to help us find out what they want."

She shook her head. She couldn't go out there. She couldn't face a crowd of angry outsiders.

"Nola, there isn't a choice." He took both her hands in his.

"You have to go out there. I've told them you'd come, and if you don't show up, people will die. Guards will die."

"Why?" The shock of Captain Ridgeway's words jolted air back into her lungs. "Why would you say I'll go out there? What could they want from me?"

"You won't be there alone. You will be surrounded by Outer Guard. I'll be nearby. We won't let them hurt you." He pulled Nola to her feet.

"What do I say?" she begged. "You can't just send me out there if I don't know what I'm supposed to say."

"There isn't time." Captain Ridgeway thrust a heavy vest into her hands. "There is nothing we can do but get out there." He pressed an I-Vent into her palm. "My guards' lives are depending on you, Nola. Don't let them down."

Captain Ridgeway wrenched open the door to the hall. The Outer Guard had already gone.

"Why me?" Nola's hands shook as she pulled on the heavy vest. "I can't offer them anything."

"You're the girl the domes went to battle for." He took her arm, holding on so tightly she could feel bruises forming as they ran up the stairs.

"That doesn't mean I can help any of them." Nola stumbled, but the captain's grip on her arm was so fierce she couldn't fall. Instead, he carried her up a few steps without even seeming to notice.

They reached the corridor where she had left Jeremy fighting with Captain Stokes.

"Jeremy." She scanned the empty hall. "I left him here."

"He'll be with the other Outer Guard. We'll meet them in the atrium."

"But what if Stokes took him away?" Nola wheezed.

"Not an option." Captain Ridgeway didn't even look worried that his son could be in trouble as he ran the rest of the way to the atrium.

The atrium was three times as high as any of the other domes and wide enough to hold at least six of the others inside it. Stored along one side were all the vehicles that belonged to the domes, always seeming out of place between the benches, trees, and paths that filled the rest of the space. In the wall right next to the vehicles was the only door to the outside world.

Work had only just been finished on the glass and on the giant door that had been damaged in the Nightland attack. The trees and grass that had been torn up had yet to be replaced, giving the place a tattered feeling. The trucks against the far wall roared to life and pulled into a line in front of the door.

The Outer Guard had already loaded themselves into the trucks, dressed in heavy riot gear, all carrying weapons.

"The sirens haven't gone off," Nola said as Captain Ridgeway steered her to the third truck in line. "People need to get to the bunkers. Why haven't the sirens gone off?"

"The sirens are under Captain Stokes' command." The captain lifted her into the high front seat of the truck before leaping up after her. "The Dome Guard are staying put. They can evacuate if the bridge gets crossed."

"But people will have more time if—"

"Use the I-Vent," Captain Ridgeway said, ignoring Nola as the trucks rumbled forward.

She held the thin silver tube up to her lips, taking a deep breath and letting the medicine fill her lungs, preventing the impurities of the outside air from contaminating her. Her panic worsened at the metallic taste the medicine left in her mouth.

Nola Kent. They want to talk to Nola Kent.

"Where's Jeremy?" Nola asked.

"With the guards," Captain Ridgeway answered, his eyes locked onto the bridge that had just come into sight.

It was easier to see the source of the blaze from outside the domes. A thousand figures standing on the far side of the bridge, holding torches, flashlights, and lanterns, making a patch of light the domes had not been able to ignore.

"Are you sure Stokes doesn't have him?" Nola said.

"Positive."

"Which truck is he in?" Her mouth had gone dry, her lips cracking as she fought to form words.

"Fifth truck. The last one in line."

The first truck in line reached the bridge and peeled off to flank the left side; the second peeled off to the right.

"Can he come here?" Nola asked as the truck carrying her and the captain slowed directly in front of the bridge. "Please, can he come with me?"

The captain studied her for a moment before speaking into his wrist. "Send Jeremy Ridgeway to the front."

Thank you. Nola couldn't manage to say the words.

He climbed out of the truck and lifted her to the ground. A line of guards ran in front of them, standing between Nola and the bridge.

Another guard ran up from behind, heading straight toward her.

"What's going on?" Jeremy asked, his voice muffled through the thick shielding of his helmet.

"Nola's going out there to talk to them, and you'll be in the escort." Captain Ridgeway rammed his own helmet onto his head.

"We can't just—"

"We can, and we are," Captain Ridgeway said. "Now you can either be in the escort or get to the back."

"Yes, sir," Jeremy barked, but Nola could hear the worry behind his words. He didn't want her going out there any more than she wanted to go herself. "She needs a helmet, sir."

"No helmet." Captain Ridgeway took Nola by the shoulders and steered her toward the bridge. "They need to be able to see who they're talking to."

He pushed her through the line of guards.

"Don't let her get past the center mark, and rifles up at all times," Captain Ridgeway shouted to the guards that filed onto either side of Nola. "Under no circumstances is there to be physical contact, and if things get nasty, the first priority is to get Magnolia Kent to safety."

"Yes, sir," the voices around them chorused.

The captain nodded and walked forward. Nola followed a step behind as did the guards that surrounded her.

Jeremy stayed right next to her, matching her every step. She wanted to reach out and hold his hand, but he gripped his weapon, pointing it at the people on the other side of the bridge.

Nola shuddered as she took the step that carried her from the road onto the bridge. The metal beneath her clanged with every footfall. The noise of the guards' heavy boots shook the air and rattled her lungs like a vicious tolling bell, counting down the steps she had left before she reached the middle of the bridge.

A line of people approached from the other side, holding torches and lanterns high in the air. They didn't have any weapons Nola could see, but if they were wolves or Vampers, they wouldn't need guns to kill the guards, or Nola.

Finally, Captain Ridgeway held up a hand, and the guards stopped as one.

The silence rang louder in Nola's ears than the clanging of the bridge had.

The group from the city stopped fifty feet away. There were twenty of them in a tight pack, all tense, ready to fight or run.

Run. Please, run.

"We were told we could speak to Nola Kent," the man at the front of the pack said from across the gap.

Torn clothes hung loosely on his frame, displaying his sinewy muscles. Even in the chill night air, the man wore short sleeves and seemed unbothered by the cold. In the dim light, Nola could barely make out the reddish hue of the man's eyes.

A werewolf.

CHAPTER SEVENTEEN

Shaking, Nola stepped forward, using every ounce of willpower she possessed to move toward the wolves.

"I'm—" She was speaking too softly. They would never be able to hear. "I'm Nola Kent!"

The man leaned forward, and Nola had the terrible feeling he was trying to catch her scent.

"Allory," the man barked, and a woman stepped forward.

Even in the darkness, Nola recognized the woman. She was the outsider who had started the fight in the Amber Dome that morning.

"Is it her?" the man asked Allory.

Looking terrified of standing so close to the man, Allory took a step sideways, squinting at Nola.

"That's her," Allory said. "That is Nola Kent."

The man smiled. "I didn't think they would actually let the little butterfly out of her cage to play at night."

"Well, I'm here." Nola took a step forward. A hand reached out and grabbed her wrist, stopping her before she could step in front of Captain Ridgeway. She knew it was Jeremy without look-ing, the way his pinky draped over her palm. He didn't want her to move away from him. She stepped to the side, closer to Jeremy and where she could properly see the pack in front of her. "What do you want from me?"

The man threw his head back and laughed. "You are better than I had hoped you would be, you wonderful little butterfly!"

The pack behind him rumbled into laughter, and the sound grew like a wave, which lapped back to the horde on the far side of the bridge, who began cheering and jeering.

"I said, what do you want!" Nola's fear dissolved in the fury of her anger.

"What do we want?" the man repeated. "What do you think I want, little butterfly?"

"How would I know?" she said. "I don't even know who you are."

"Lucifer, at your service." The man bowed deeply.

"I don't believe you," Nola said. "You know my name, why can't I know yours?"

"Lucifer is what I am." He smiled. "A fallen angel who brings darkness to all. What is a name meant to be if not a description of what we are?"

"Fine, *Lucifer*," she spat the name, "what do you want from me?"

Get off the bridge. Get off the bridge and get back to the domes. Being locked in the bunker is better than being on this bridge with the wolves.

"We want what all of us want." Lucifer raised both hands in the air, inciting cheers from the people behind him. He tipped his head to the side and sneered, looking like a rabid wolf that wanted nothing more than to bite. "We want food," Lucifer growled. "We want medicine. We want our fair share of the riches you've got in the domes."

"We don't have riches." Nola laughed loudly, though her heart still fought to burst out of her chest. "I don't know why you think we do."

"We don't want gold and jewels, butterfly, we want food. And I know you have that." Lucifer grabbed Allory under one arm, lifting her off her feet. "Allory here told us about your food. Rows and rows of food just waiting to be eaten. Isn't that right, Allory?"

"Yes," Allory whimpered. "I saw it, worked in just one of the domes, and there's more food there than I've ever seen."

"Thank you, Allory." Lucifer let go of Allory's arm, and she crumpled to the ground where she lay shaking, not even attempting to stand back up. "You have food. You are hoarding food and watching the city starve. We'd always thought it, but now thanks to Allory"—he kicked Allory in the stomach, and, with a cry of pain, she rolled to face the sky—"well, now we know that you have stores of food. That you filthy Domers in your glass castle high on the hill just like watching the rest of us starve. Well, we say *enough*!" Lucifer punched the air, and a roar soared from the far side of the bridge.

"So tonight, we eat!" Lucifer bared his teeth, which shone white in the moonlight.

The rustle of the guards behind her sent a shiver up Nola's spine.

"The only question is do we eat your food, or you?"

The snarls of the pack carried over Lucifer's words.

The domes could feed all these people for one week, maybe two, but then there would be nothing left. All of them would starve.

She glanced toward Captain Ridgeway, but his face was hidden behind his visor.

"Me personally?" Nola asked. "I don't think there's enough of me to go around."

The pack howled with laughter.

"Not just you, my beautiful butterfly." Lucifer took a step forward. Each of the guards pointed their rifle at his chest. He spread his arms wide and took another step forward. "We'll eat all of you. Tear the flesh from your bones and have the freshest, tenderest meat any of us has ever tasted."

"But that still doesn't answer my first question." Nola pulled her hand from Jeremy's grip and stepped in front of Captain Ridgeway. The sound of bodies shifting caught her ear, but she didn't dare turn to look. "Why did you want me out here? I have no authority in the domes, I don't know how much food we've got, and even if I wanted to give it to you, I couldn't. I am no one. Why would you want to talk to me in the middle of the night on a bridge over a rancid river?"

"Because I've heard stories about Nola Kent, the butterfly that flew into Nightland." Lucifer's red eyes bore into hers. "The butterfly that didn't want to kill the Vampers, who helped them get medicine."

Nola's breath caught in her chest. If this man knew she had stolen, then she should walk into the city now and save the Council the trouble of having to formally banish her.

"I can't give you anything." The warmth had drained from her body, stolen by the wind. She couldn't feel her hands as they shook, and each ragged breath stole heat from her lungs.

"You wouldn't let the slaves you master fight," Lucifer said. "You protected them, kept them in the warm."

"They are not our slaves," Nola said.

"We are all slaves to the ones who have the food. The babies who cry from hunger and the old that waste away rather than take a crust of bread that might save the young. We are all slaves to the death that lurks over this city, and you in the glass castle have mastered that death. With your food and medicine. The acid rains can't burn you, and the winters can't freeze you. And the ones who have mastered death are masters of us all."

"That doesn't make sense!" she shouted. "I didn't let my people fight, so what? I kept them inside the domes, but why do you care? What the hell have they got to do with you?"

"My beautiful butterfly, you are the only soul in the glass castle of murderers who has ever shown compassion. The rest all turn away from the diseased and the dying. The light from their mythical bright future blinds them to the darkness. But you've seen what lies in the shadows, and we will haunt you for the rest of your days."

"I still can't help you," Nola said as thoughts of desperate children grasped at the edges of her mind. "I wish I could. I wish there was enough for everyone, but there isn't. Even if we wanted to feed the city, we couldn't."

"I think the butterfly is lying. That the only one from the glass who can see truth has turned to lies to survive. Or"—he turned to look at the woman lying on the ground—"Allory has. Are you lying to me, Allory? Stores of food, you said. Long tunnels with places to sleep, you said."

"It's true," Allory whimpered. "Everything is there up the hill. I swear to you."

Lucifer swept his gaze from Allory to Nola.

"One of my girls is lying. And one knows the price of lying," Lucifer snarled, "which makes me think it's probably her." He leaned over Allory who lay sobbing on the ground.

"Stop!" Nola shouted. "There is food. But not enough for everyone. And it takes time, a lot of time, to grow more. If we fed half of you even, there wouldn't be enough for anyone to survive. Please believe me!"

Lucifer grabbed Allory's arm, wrenching her to her feet.

"I wish I could help you, but I can't." Nola reached toward Allory, wishing she were strong enough to run forward and snatch her from Lucifer's arms, but he pulled her closer, tracing the curve of her neck with his nose as he scented her skin.

"The domes can't save the city," Nola said, "but we might be able to do something, figure out something. Nightland had gardens, gardens that grew good food." She took another step forward, pulling Lucifer's eyes from Allory back to herself. "And they had a way to filter the rain water, and keep the acid rain off the plants. I'll bet you knew that, though," Nola shouted as loudly as she could, hoping the people on the far side of the bridge could hear her. "Nightland found a way to feed the children. And they did it on their own without help from the domes. I saw the garden. Maybe some of you did, too. Is that why you're so angry now, because Nightland abandoned you? Because they aren't here to feed you anymore?"

"No one wants the Vamper scum on our streets!" A man behind Lucifer spat on the ground, and as one, the pack tipped their heads back and howled at the sky.

Nola fought to swallow the knot of fear in her throat as the sound vibrated the metal under her feet.

"Fine!" Nola shouted as soon as the howling began to fade. "Fine! You don't want Nightland's help. But what they did was amazing. And I'll do whatever I can to help you rebuild what they had. So you can grow your own food."

"And how many will be dead by the time the food grows?" Lucifer said.

"How many will die if we eat what we can't replace?" She took another step forward. The sound of boots on metal followed her. "I'll find a way to help, but I can't give you anything tonight."

"So we should wait and starve while you go home to your nice bed and full belly?" Lucifer stepped forward, gripping Allory's neck and dragging her with him. "Tell me how that sounds fair, little butterfly?"

"It isn't fair," Nola said. "The world ending isn't fair. Nothing is fair. But you wanted to talk to me, and this is the best I can do."

"No, little butterfly, it isn't." Lucifer smiled. "The best you can do is for my city to be fed. We'll eat our fill tonight, and when there's nothing left of the Domers but bloody bones, we'll have your nice beds to rest in and all the dome food to eat."

"Please don't," Nola said. "How many people will die if you try to fight us?"

"Butterfly"—with a grin on his face, Lucifer leaned down as though to kiss Allory's neck—"we're already dead."

"No!" Nola screamed, but her cry was covered by Allory's. The shriek lasted for only a moment before a spurt of blood sprayed the ground.

Someone wrapped a hand around Nola's arm, but she didn't turn to see who had yanked her backward. The pack rushed forward, hiding Allory behind their surging mass.

Poor Allory.

"Get her out of here!" Captain Ridgeway's voice cut over the screams as she was dragged through the front line of guards. As soon as she was behind the line, they began firing on the mob that had rushed toward them. The people at the back of the bridge were piling on, joining the fight. There were too many of them for the guards to face. Sheer numbers would overwhelm the domes.

Pure light ripped through the night with a *bang*. A weight struck Nola in the chest, sending her flying as someone pulled her beneath them, shielding her from the terrible light. The bridge under her gave an awful lurch and somewhere far away people screamed. The noise of the screams was muted in her ears, tiny bugs trying to cut through the terrible ringing.

"Get up!" Jeremy's voice shouted. The one who had protected her from the light.

Of course it's Jeremy.

"Are you hurt?" he yelled, sounding like he was underwater, his words almost too muffled for her to understand. But he didn't wait for her to answer. People ran toward them, away from a fire at the end of the bridge.

But the bridge now ended far before the other side of the river. Half of the bridge had disappeared leaving only jagged bits of flaming metal reaching toward the city.

A blaze illuminated the far bank of the river. Bodies lay near the shore, some of the corpses on fire.

Jeremy pulled her farther away, into the crowd of guards charging forward to meet the wolves who had made it to their side of the bridge before the light.

Explosion. That's the word for it. I saw an explosion.

They were behind the last truck now. The domes glittered up the hill, looking so perfect. There was no sign of the explosion that had broken the domes. That had been mended. But the burning bodies on the shore could never be mended.

"Nola. Nola!" Jeremy shouted, taking her by the shoulders and shaking her. "Nola!"

"Yes," she said, wanting so badly to take off Jeremy's helmet so she could see his face.

"Nola, I need you to run for the domes."

Guns sounded behind them.

How many wolves had gotten over the bridge?

"I need you to run home and don't stop until you're at the door. They'll let you in."

"Come with me, please!" She grabbed Jeremy's hands. "I can't go without you!"

"You have to, Nola. Keep your head down and run. I'll be at your house by sunrise, I promise you."

"No, please!" She couldn't lose him. She wouldn't.

An agonizing scream cut through the sounds of the fight.

"I love you, Nola. Now run!"

"I love you," Nola whispered before turning toward the glass castle and running up the hill.

CHAPTER EIGHTEEN

Tears and sweat mixed on her face. The sounds of fighting didn't fade as she ran up the hill. They followed her like a demon, keeping pace with her every step.

She had left him. She had left Jeremy in the dark, fighting werewolves.

Home by sunrise. He'll be home by sunrise.

Screams chased her. Terrible, terrified screams. Something like a snarl followed. And then—

Pop, pop, pop.

Such a tiny little noise that could mean the end of someone's life.

Home by sunrise. He'll be home by sunrise.

The air burned Nola's lungs as she ran up the hill. Her legs protested every step. Something warm and sticky dripped down her shoulder. But she didn't dare look to see if it was her own blood that smeared her flesh or someone else's.

The door to the atrium came into sight. Twelve guards stood out front, weapons trained on the darkness around them. The Dome Guard should be down fighting with the Outer Guard on the bridge. Why were they standing in the darkness while others fought?

"Help!" Nola tried to scream, but the words barely made it past her lips. "Help!"

Two of the guards ran toward her, their rifles pointed at her chest.

"They need help down at the bridge!" she panted.

"Freeze!" one of the guards shouted.

Nola ran faster, trying to get away from whatever was chasing her.

"I said freeze!"

She stopped so suddenly she nearly tipped over.

"Please...they need help...at the bridge!" Nola begged between gasps.

"Magnolia Kent?" one of the guards asked.

"There are wolves on the bridge," Nola said as a guard shone his light on her vest.

"Take off the vest," the first guard said.

Nola pulled off the vest and dropped it onto the ground. She didn't need protection. She needed them to listen. "There was an explosion on the bridge. Guards are hurt."

"The Outer Guard can take care themselves." He pointed his light at her shoulder. "You're injured. We need to get you inside."

"I'm fine." Nola stepped back as one of the guards reached for her.

But another guard caught her tightly around the waist and carried her to the door.

"No, please. I'm fine. You have to help them!" Nola fought against the man's grip.

"Our orders are not to leave the perimeter of the domes." The guard punched a code into the door, and it *whooshed* open. Fresh air spilled out of the atrium, and hands grabbed Nola, pulling her inside before the doors had fully opened.

"We found her, sir."

Captain Stokes stood just inside the door, glaring at Nola.

"Keep them from getting near the glass," Captain Stokes shouted as the door lowered.

"But they need to get to the guards on the bridge!" Nola wrenched her arms free from the hands that held her.

"Captain Ridgeway chose to take his men to the bridge. Their blood is on his hands," Captain Stokes said. "I will not have the blood of my men on mine."

"And if the wolves get past them? If they break through the glass again?"

"My men will do their duty and protect the domes," Stokes said. "Fighting the people across the river is not what we have been assigned to do. As Captain Ridgeway has made clear again and again. Get her medical help."

A guard standing next to Stokes raised his wrist to his mouth and began muttering.

"You fought with them in the city," Nola pleaded. "You did it then. Why not now?"

"Because my men are not in the business of slaughter." Hatred twisted Stokes' face. "We protect the lives in these domes. What the Outer Guard do is on their own damned heads. Get her to the bunker."

"No!" she screamed as two guards reached toward her. "I just watched a woman's neck get ripped open and a bridge explode. I tried to stop this from happening, and I failed. I'm not waiting underground to see if the monsters make it to our door."

Stokes eyed her for a moment. "Let her stay."

A woman in a white coat ran into the atrium, emergency medical bag in hand.

Nola didn't flinch as the doctor tore away her sleeve. Stokes was still studying her, and she wouldn't look away.

"You never could have stopped it, Miss Kent," Stokes finally said, as though he had spent the last five minutes searching for words. "Nothing you could have done would have stopped the bridge from burning." He pushed the words from his throat as if every syllable cost him an enormous effort. Without waiting for her reply, he turned and walked to the back of the atrium, toward the high concrete tower that loomed over the domes.

Nola turned back to the glass. The bridge was barely visible in the darkness, only flames marked the bloody expanse.

"We need to get you down to the medical unit," the doctor said.

Nola didn't register the doctor pulling at her skin until she looked down. The blood on her arm had been hers. A piece of something was lodged in her bicep. The longer she stared at it, the more she realized she was looking at her own arm. Then the pain began.

"We need to get your arm taken care of," the doctor said. "Did you hit your head? Are you dizzy?"

"I'm fine." Nola shook her head as though the movement would emphasize how fine she was.

"We need to run some tests." The doctor shone a bright light into her eyes.

"I'm not leaving." Nola looked back to the bridge. "I'm not leaving while he's fighting."

The doctor swore, unpacking her medical bag, muttering darkly about guards allowing things to interfere with her patient's care.

"Have you at least used an I-Vent?" the doctor snapped as she pulled bits of shining black metal from Nola's arm.

Pain surged through her with each little scrap that was removed. She savored every sting. She deserved to be in pain. People were dying down the hill because she had failed.

"I-Vent," the doctor shouted, as though Nola were deaf.

Fishing in her back pocket with her good hand, Nola pulled out the tiny tube and took a deep breath, never taking her eyes from the bridge.

The fighting had moved closer to the domes in the ten

minutes she had been inside. Nola laughed. A panicked chuckle that caught in her throat.

"And she's lost her mind," the doctor muttered.

"I liked that last doctor I saw better," Nola said.

"I don't think you're appreciating—"

"You're fixing a few broken inches of skin on my arm, and wolves could kill us all by morning."

A blaze lit the far side of the bridge. Something large had been sacrificed to the inferno. Like the city had lit a fire to shed light on the sins of the battle.

With a *hiss* from a canister, the doctor sprayed something that burned Nola's arm.

"I am going to have a lot more patients before the end of the night," the doctor said, dry fear crackling in her voice. "I'd really like to be done with you before they get here."

She smeared blue goo onto Nola's arm. As if on cue, a truck rumbled up the hill.

Her heart leapt.

It's over!

But no, it couldn't be. There were still people moving at the bottom of the hill. Still tiny sparks of firing weapons lighting the night.

"And that will be my wounded." The doctor wrapped a bandage around Nola's arm. "I don't care where the hell you go, but if you actually care about the wounded guards who are about to be coming through this door, get the hell out of the atrium. Go to the bunkers, go to your own bed, I couldn't care less. But I will not allow you to stay here and be in my way."

The vents rumbled as the door opened.

"Take care of them." Nola ran to the far side of the atrium and down into the tunnels.

He'll be home by sunrise.

Nola tore through the tunnel to Bright Dome. From her roof

she would be able to see if the fighting came closer, even if she couldn't see the bridge.

Bright Dome was empty, abandoned by all the residents who had fled to the bunker. For a moment, she wondered if her mother had looked for her. Had asked the guard who kept them all trapped where Magnolia Kent had gone. But her mother probably hadn't gone to the bunker. She would have snuck away to be down with her seeds, making sure no panicked person or malicious intruder dared damage them.

Nola leapt up the two steps to her door and burst through the kitchen without bothering to turn on the lights. She sprinted up the stairs and into her room. Something soft tangled around her feet, and she fell forward, screaming as her hurt arm took the impact.

"Leave me alone!" Nola shouted, kicking away whoever was trying to trap her. But there was no one hiding in the shadows or pinning her down. The soft, white towel she had dropped what seemed like a lifetime ago lay on the floor, now stained by her boots.

Panting, she pushed herself up. The pain in her arm had become impossible to ignore, but she had to see what was happening. Stepping up on the windowsill, she couldn't stop the scream of pain that wrenched from her throat as she pulled herself onto the roof.

The cool, soft moss, terribly unlike everything happening in the world, cradled her cheek. She shouldn't be sitting on something so gentle and familiar while Jeremy was outside fighting for his life.

The fire on the city side of the bridge had grown, reaching the buildings that sat along the water. The smoke from the flames clouded the sky, obscuring the river's edge.

Nola swore, screaming at the flames, and the smoke, and the wolves and explosions.

There was still movement on the remaining half of the shattered bridge.

How many wolves had made it to their side of the explosion? Surely the fighting would be over soon. And the rest would be stuck in the fires they had created on the far side of the river. There would be no guards going into the city to try and save people from the flames. There was no way across.

The river ran with a swift current, and the water had been contaminated from years of industrial pollution. Even if someone were strong enough to make it from the city to the domes, submerging in the water would be a death sentence.

But would it be a death sentence to the wolves?

Nola shut her eyes against the night, and dark, imagined shapes swam through the water that shone in her mind.

She wouldn't be able to see them swimming. The distance, smoke, and darkness all prevented that.

But if they could. If they swam over. If there are boats hidden in the city...

Then Jeremy will fight them, too.

Nola opened her eyes and looked back toward the river. Trucks drove back up the hill. And bright, fake lights bathed the remnants of the bridge. She wanted to leap off the roof and run to the atrium, to search every truck for Jeremy as they came in. If he was injured, she should sit by his bed just as she had before. But the doctor had told her to stay out of the way. That it would be safer for the wounded.

Digging her fingers into the moss, Nola anchored herself to the roof as though expecting a wind to blow her away.

Her arm throbbed with every beat of her heart.

Home by sunrise. He promised. He'll be home by sunrise.

CHAPTER NINETEEN

Hours passed. Or maybe just a few minutes. She didn't know what time she had been taken to the bridge, so there was no way to know how long the wait for the sky to turn gray would be.

Her fingers went numb from gripping the moss on the roof long before the faint part of the sky visible through the smoke lightened.

Tears ran down Nola's cheeks, but she couldn't brush them away. Her arms were too heavy to lift to her face.

There were still people moving on the bridge. In the dim light she could see them like ants, carrying and pushing things from the broken bridge to the water.

Bodies. They were throwing bodies into the water. If they were disposing of the dead, the danger must be over.

Jeremy was hurt. He must be, or he would have come for her. Unless he was out with the people left on the bridge. Or maybe he thought she was down in one of the bunkers and had gone there. Or maybe...

Nola couldn't let herself finish that maybe.

I'll be home by sunrise.

He promised.

Orange tinted the sky. A sad, dusty orange tainted by the fire, unable to match the crackling brightness of the flames through the haze that coated the world.

A blanket that suffocates us all.

Her breath came in quick gasps. She would suffocate on the roof. The world itself would smother her, and she deserved it.

A heaving sob broke free, and then another. She wept on the roof, staring at the sun, willing it to stop its relentless rise, knowing she would never have that power.

Home by sunrise.

The edge of the sun burst free from the horizon.

"No, no, no!" Nola railed against the sun, but it wouldn't listen. "Stop! Please stop!"

"Nola!" a voice shouted from the far side of Bright Dome. "Nola!"

She had nearly missed the sound in her screaming.

"Nola!"

Painfully, she pried her fingers from the moss and crawled to the other side of the roof where she could see the rest of the dome.

"Jeremy." His name came out as a whisper through her tears. "Jeremy!"

He ran toward her house. His stride long and even. Blood and dirt marked his uniform, but relief brightened his face as soon as he saw her.

Scrambling back across the roof, Nola dropped over the edge and through her window, all pain forgotten as Jeremy's heavy boots pounded up the stairs.

"Nola, are you hurt?" the words were out of his mouth before he was in her room, but she didn't answer. She had already thrown herself into his arms and was kissing him with everything she possessed.

Explosions and blood melted away. Death and fear didn't matter. Jeremy was alive and holding her.

The room didn't sway, and she didn't want it to. She wanted to hold on tighter, to pull herself closer so no one would ever be able to separate them again. There was no more her or him. No difference between them at all.

His fingers found skin at her waist and drifted up her back. She gasped at the warmth of his touch, craving more. Her heart raced as he hungrily grasped her side with his hand. Suddenly, her shirt became a hateful thing, another horrible barrier between them. Nola eased her hold on him only enough to reach for the edge of her shirt but as soon as she moved, Jeremy was there pulling it off for her.

Blood rose to her cheeks not with embarrassment, but anticipation. He let go of her for a moment to take off his heavy guard's vest. But that brief moment felt like an eternity. Like he would fall away from her completely.

She pulled herself closer to him. Kissing him again as though trying to prove he was still alive. With only his thin guard's shirt between them, his heart racing pressed against hers. The taste of him, the feel of his heat radiating through her, washed away all the cold fear that filled her.

"Nola," Jeremy whispered, and her heart soared. He wasn't saying a name, but a prayer that they would always be together. That he would always hold her tight, and the demons of the outside world would never again come between them.

Fingers trembling, Nola undid the buttons of his shirt, letting her chest press to his. She slid his shirt away without looking.

In one movement that sent her heart bounding from her chest, Jeremy scooped her into his arms and carried her to the bed. Laying her down gently, he gazed at her. His brown eyes smiling down at her. She reached for him, pulling him closer. The light from the sunrise shone through the window, casting an orange light on Jeremy's bare chest. A red mark glistened on his arm. Surrounded by dried blood, the cut looked like a weeks-old gash, already through the first horrible stages of healing.

Nola gasped, and her world shattered.

CHAPTER TWENTY

"What's wrong?" Jeremy asked, reaching down toward Nola, but she swatted his hand away, falling off the bed in her desperate scramble to get away from him.

"Don't touch me!" Nola's back slammed into the edge of her dresser, sending a wave of pain through her spine. "Ouch!"

Jeremy reached for her again. "Nola, be careful."

"I said don't touch me!" she screamed, groping her way up the desk, not looking away from Jeremy.

"Nola, I'm sorry." Jeremy's face crumpled. He tucked his hands behind him as though trying to prove he wouldn't reach for her again.

But the movement tightened the skin on his arm, making the red line of freshly healed flesh even more apparent.

"I shouldn't have done that. I shouldn't have pushed you so fast, I'm sorry."

"How could you?" she whispered. "How could you?"

She wanted to say more, to scream and rage, but the words wouldn't come.

"I love you, Nola. I want to be with you." Desperation filled his eyes. "Please, Nola. I'm sorry. I would never hurt you."

"What did they give you?" Nola asked. "Where did you get it?"

"What are you..." Jeremy's gaze followed Nola's shaking hand as she pointed to his arm. He swallowed, his pulse throbbed in his neck. "It's not what you think."

"It's exactly what I think," she spat. "I've seen people heal like that before. I saw it happen to me in Nightland. What did you take? Vamp? Lycan? Or maybe you got lucky and found some ReVamp?"

"It's not any of that," he said, his voice dry and shallow. "I would never take any of that."

"Then what? What name did you decide to call the drug in order to make yourself feel better about using it?"

"Graylock," Jeremy whispered. "We call it Graylock. They gave it to all the men in the Outer Guard."

"What?" Nola stumbled as the room spun.

He lunged forward and caught her an inch before she hit the floor.

She pushed on his chest with both hands, trying to get him to let go, but he didn't seem to notice.

He set her easily back on her feet. "We had to take it, Nola." Jeremy backed as far away from her as the tiny room would allow. "With Vampers and wolves on the streets, the Outer Guard didn't stand a chance without it."

"So you became them." It was all falling away, one sheet of lies at a time, and the shattering rang through her mind, jumbling her thoughts. "You did what you hate the Vampers for doing. You changed your DNA. Made yourselves monsters just like them."

"No. Not like them. We have better scientists here than the outsiders could ever hope for. Graylock makes us stronger and faster. We can heal and fight, but I'm still me. It didn't change anything about my mind. No bloodlust, no anger. I can still eat, and go in the sun, and I still love you."

"How could your father allow this? The domes were built to preserve the human race. Without contamination from the outside world. If this drug changes the way your body works, it changes what you are. You might as well be a vampire!" The words tore from her throat.

"Please don't shout, Nola. People can't know about this. You aren't supposed to know about this. No one can find out that you know."

"Why?" She crossed her arms, covering her bare chest. "Because if the Council finds out what the Outer Guard have been doing—"

"The Council knows," Jeremy said. "The Incorporation itself gave approval for the research."

"No. No, the Incorporation built the domes to preserve humans, not create monsters. They would never let this happen."

"They approved the research and the Outer Guard's use of Graylock. That's why Stokes has been such an evil little varmint. Our guys can do things his can't. The Dome Guard and Outer Guard aren't equal anymore."

"Because the Dome Guard are protecting what the domes were built for." Stokes' words suddenly made sense. Why should he send his men out to bleed when the Outer Guard could be stabbed and heal without any treatment?

"We take Graylock to protect the domes," Jeremy pleaded. "We couldn't fight the city dwellers before, but now we can. We can fight the wolves and live. They were slaughtering us before. We had to do something."

"My father was an Outer Guard, and he never injected himself with filth to do his job."

"And they killed him," Jeremy said, so softly she could barely hear. His words were without malice or taunt. Just cold, painful truth. "And I would have died, too. I wouldn't have survived the werewolf riot without Graylock. It saved my life."

Nola's mind raced back to a filing cabinet filled with black vials and a needle filled with black sliding into Jeremy's chest.

"They started giving it to the Outer Guard right before the

raid on Nightland, and we still lost six men. We would have lost a lot more without it. And the attack on the domes, it would have been a massacre without Graylock."

"If it keeps you strong and healthy, then we should send it to the outsiders," Nola said. "Graylock could be the cure they've been looking for. You could save people!"

"We're saving the domes." Jeremy took a tiny step forward. "If all of those people had it, we wouldn't be able to stop an attack."

He was right. She knew he was right, and she hated herself for it.

"But the domes were built to preserve the future," Nola said. "That's bigger than who can fight better. It's about protecting future generations. None of the Outer Guard will be able to have children now. What's the point of—"

"But *we* will be able to have children." Warmth filled Jeremy's voice. "They figured all that out. Before any of us were allowed to take Graylock, they took samples from us. We could still have healthy children."

Nola backed into the wall, leaning on it for support as her head spun.

"Not now, not for a long time. But the doctors"—Jeremy ran his hands through his hair—"they have everything stored, and when, I mean, *if* we ever wanted kids, they could do it."

"With doctors." Nola's lips numbed. The feeling drifted down to her fingers, then coated her whole body. "Doctors to put things inside of me, but not Gentry. That's why she left, isn't it? You said they gave Graylock to the men, but she couldn't have it. She needed to be kept *pure for breeding*." She spat the words, hating the feeling of them in her mouth.

Jeremy pressed the heels of his hands into his eyes. "She fought for it. She wanted to take Graylock, but they wouldn't let her. They couldn't risk losing her DNA for procreation."

Bile rose in her throat. An animal for breeding. That was how they had treated Gentry. Strong, trained, brave Gentry. "How could they expect her to let the rest of her family take it and not be strong enough to protect them? But it doesn't matter what the Council wanted. The domes lost her anyway."

"She can be a guard in a different set of domes," he said. "We're the only ones who use Graylock. We're the only ones who have fighting this bad. We had to do it to survive."

Kieran had said nearly the same thing to her on a roof high above the decaying city. He was drowning in his own body, and ReVamp had saved his life. Had given him a chance to help others...and betray Nola.

She shut her eyes tight, shuddering at the thought of Jeremy and Kieran being anything like the same.

"Nola, I love you."

She sensed him moving closer but didn't shrink away.

"I love you more than anything. I took my first dose the day we raided Nightland to try and get you back. I never wanted to take something like Graylock, but I had to do it. I had to do whatever gave me the best chance of protecting you." His fingers brushed the bandage on her arm. "And even with Graylock, I still couldn't keep you safe."

"An explosion can kill Vampers and werewolves." Nola opened her eyes. Jeremy was only a few inches from her. She leaned into his chest, willing it to feel the same as it had a few minutes ago when she hadn't known about the chemicals racing through his veins with every heartbeat. "A severed neck or a broken heart, it'll kill a Vamper or a wolf. It would get you, too." She shuddered and unfolded her arms. Letting her skin press into his.

"I know." Jeremy wrapped his arms around her. "But I still should have been able to protect you."

"They blew up a bridge. There's no way anyone could have imagined they would sacrifice their own people like that."

Nola felt Jeremy stiffen before the words rumbled in his chest.

"They didn't blow up the bridge, Nola. We did."

CHAPTER TWENTY-ONE

The sound began far at the back of Nola's brain. A terrible screaming that had no words. One high-pitched, piercing screech that floated further and further forward, fighting to block out Jeremy's voice.

"The bomb was planted under the bridge a long time ago." Jeremy held her up by the shoulders, pleading and fear painting his face. "To make sure the outsiders didn't cross the bridge and overwhelm the domes. If we had seen Nightland coming, we could have stopped them, too, but they got over some other way. If we hadn't blown up the bridge, those people would have come across and attacked us. We had no other choice."

The screaming in her head had grown too loud now. She couldn't hear his words at all. He was talking fast, his lips forming important phrases she couldn't hear over the terrible shrieking. Nola watched his lips, trying to find something in the pattern of their movement that would make sense. That would mean her home hadn't just blown up a bridge filled with people.

Bile shot up into her mouth. Shoving past Jeremy, she ran for the toilet. Her stomach threw up the revulsion that overwhelmed her, but the screaming in her head wouldn't stop.

Jeremy knelt next to her, holding her up as she trembled and heaved. The noise told her he was shouting something, but it didn't matter. What he was shouting about didn't matter. How could it matter more than...than.... How many people had been at the edge of the bridge when it exploded? Fifty?

No, more. It was more.

The shriek in her head had learned to speak words.

You saw them running toward you. More than a hundred. Running toward you. Running toward your home until they were burned up in an instant.

"I was a diversion," Nola said as the screaming in her head stopped, leaving her with deafening quiet. "Your dad knew I wouldn't be able to talk to them. He knew I wouldn't be able to stop it. I was just supposed to buy them time. So they could be sure everything was in place." She seized Jeremy's face. "Tell me I wasn't a diversion. Tell me I didn't help you kill those people."

"They would have killed us." Jeremy pressed Nola's hands to his cheeks. "They would have come over here and killed all of us. Ripped out our throats, you heard him."

"They lied to me. They used me," Nola whimpered as the room swayed.

"Nola..." Jeremy reached to pull her closer, but she pushed herself away, falling backward onto the floor and hitting her head hard on the corner of the shower.

"Nola."

"Don't touch me!" she shouted, jumping to her feet even as the room around her swam dangerously.

"Nola, you're bleeding." Jeremy reached again to steady her.

"Get out of my house. Get the hell out of here. And you and your Graylock and your lies and your bombs stay the hell away from me!"

He looked as though she had slapped him hard across the face. Blinking dazedly, he stared at her like he thought she might come to her senses if only he froze long enough for her to sort out what it was she might be thinking.

"Get out," Nola growled. "Get out, get out, get out!"

But he wouldn't move. He stood like a confused statue in her bathroom, which smelled of sour and blood. She pushed around him, snatched her blood-stained shirt from the floor, and ran down the stairs, leaning heavily on the walls as her head spun. She didn't stop to close the door behind her or wonder how long it would be until her mother came home and found blood on the corner of the shower.

Half-formed plans swam in her head. Her feet carried her out through the grass of Bright Dome, off the path, and behind a willow tree. The hole in the glass had been sealed. There was no way out here. But she would have to find one. The ones left to suffer had come for the glass castle, and they wouldn't stop until the river ran red with blood. When that day came, she would not be left in the domes to watch it.

Smoke covered the skyline of the city, blocking out the places where families would be mourning. And where wolves would be plotting their revenge.

Nola pressed her head to the cool glass. The morning light still hadn't stolen the chill of the night away. Warm blood trickled down her neck. There were things to be done, and she knew where to go first.

CHAPTER TWENTY-TWO

Nola waited in the hall of the medical wing for nearly an hour. There were no doctors or Outer Guard in sight. It would have seemed strange or even ominous just a short while ago. But the deep, black Graylock couldn't be injected where Domers could see, and the Outer Guard would be able to heal on their own anyway.

The hall lights had gotten bright before Doctor Mullins finally arrived in the corridor, looking tired and pulling on a fresh, white coat.

She looked at Nola for a moment, blinking as though batting away fatigue. "Magnolia, how can I help you?"

Nola let go of the bandage she had been pressing to the back of her head. "My head won't stop bleeding." She gave a crooked smile.

Doctor Mullins rushed over. "Why on earth didn't someone see you already?" Glancing briefly at Nola's head, she took her arm and led her to the door of one of the examining rooms, punching in a code before the door slid open.

"Someone looked at my arm," Nola said, deliberately not looking at the glass cases in the corner. "But when I got home, I got dizzy and hit my head. I didn't want to interrupt while all the doctors were downstairs helping the injured Outer Guard."

"Well, that was considerate of you, but head wounds are nothing to be trifled with. Especially with..." Doctor Mullins paused for a moment, then spun to face the cabinet in the corner. "Well, those who have had so much physical trauma to deal with lately."

"I'm sorry," Nola muttered, watching as Doctor Mullins punched in yet another code to open the cabinet.

3733

The cabinet popped open.

"I didn't think it mattered that much. I just couldn't get the bleeding to stop."

"We'll get you cleaned up in no time, but you really do need to be careful."

She waited patiently as Doctor Mullins shined a light into her eyes, sprayed things that stung onto her flesh, and tugged at the broken skin.

"I'm so sorry," Nola said as the doctor rubbed cool goo into her hair, "but could you maybe ask my mom to walk me home? I'm just..." She waited, hoping the doctor would sympathetically interrupt her. She didn't. "I'm not feeling great about being alone. I'd like it if my mom could come and get me."

Nola held her breath as she waited.

The doctor's stern face finally crumpled. "I'll go and grab your mom. She'll be down in seeds?"

"Yes." Nola smiled. "I'd call for her, but I'm sure she won't answer, not after having to go back to the bunker."

"I'll go find your mom." Doctor Mullins wagged a finger in an unintimidating way. "But don't let it get around that I'll run all over the domes looking for truant parents."

"Thank you!" she called as soon as the doctor was out the door.

3733

Nola jumped off the bed and ran for the cabinet. Her fingers shook as she punched in the number, but as soon as the final three was pressed, the metal doors popped open.

She stood frozen for a few moments, staring at the vast array of vials and tubs, bottles and packages. She tried to read the names, but she didn't know what half of them meant.

Hands shaking, Nola reached into the very back of the rows, careful not to disturb the order of the perfectly aligned front bottles.

Three bottles of nutrient pills, five I-Vents. Three familiar-looking silver vials she had been injected with when a flu swept through the domes four years earlier. Tubs of the goo the doctors spread on wounds to help them heal. A few packs of bandages.

She shoved the vials into the ankles of her boots, the bandages into the waist of her pants, and the bottles into her pockets.

How much more could she fit into her clothes without the doctor noticing? What would she need? She grabbed three vials of blue pills her mother had given her before for headaches and closed the cabinet.

Kieran would have done it better. He would have known what each of the names on the bottles meant and what they were used for. But Kieran had left her and betrayed her. Jeremy had lied to her and used her.

Her whole body shook as she moved back to the bed in the middle of the room. There was no one left to trust, only people to save.

Nola stared at her hands as she counted the seconds before Doctor Mullins would return. Lenora Kent wouldn't come easily. She wouldn't hear that her daughter had been hurt and come running. She would hem and haw. Be sure to check all of her specimens one last time. Assign a person to watch her computer and make sure it didn't shut down while she was away. The automatic computer alerts from PAM were never enough for her. She would want someone there watching, protecting her precious seeds.

The vials in her boots seemed to burn her skin, shouting to the domes that Nola Kent was a traitor. But the sirens didn't sound, and the lights didn't flash. So she counted until her mother arrived.

"Nola." Lenora burst through the door, looking harassed after 672 seconds. "What happened to you?"

Nola smiled to herself, swallowing the urge to laugh. "I almost got blown up on the bridge, and then hit my head really hard at home. So, a little blood and a lot of trauma."

"What?" Lenora looked at Dr. Mullins as though expecting her to say delusions were a symptom of Nola's head wound. "You were on that bridge? How in the ever-loving hell did you get out there? And what do you mean *blown up*?"

"Can I tell you at home?" Nola said.

"How did you get outside the domes? And where did you hit your head?"

Nola smiled apologetically at Doctor Mullins who stayed plastered to the side of the room as Nola's mother led her out into the hall.

"And you can't possibly tell me you had anything to do with what happened outside. I've been told there were werewolves." Lenora took Nola by the arm and dragged her up the stairs. "How could you have gotten to the bridge in the first place?"

"Captain Ridgeway set me up." Nola expected a shot of pain to fly through her chest. But there was nothing. Only a vast emptiness in the place where the pain should have been. "He made me negotiate with the wolves. Made me think there was a chance to make sure no one died. And then he blew up the bridge with me standing on it. With a hundred people running across it. He's a liar and a killer, and I never want to see him or Jeremy again."

"What?" Lenora stopped in the middle of the hall.

Nola sidestepped her and kept walking toward Bright Dome.

"They used me to buy time to kill people. And I hate them for it." She didn't look back to see if her mother was following.

She had reached the steps to Bright Dome when heavy running footfalls caught up to her.

"Nola, honey…" Lenora grabbed her daughter's arm. "That can't be what they meant to do."

"It was, Mom." Nola took her mother's hand. "Please don't pretend you don't believe me. I think you knew what the Ridgeways were capable of long before I did."

"I'm so sorry." Lenora shook her head, her fingers pressed over her lips. "What can I do?"

"Keep Jeremy away from me, and let me live my life away from him." It sounded so ridiculously simple when she said it like that.

"The Ridgeway family is no longer welcome in our home." Lenora chased Nola up the stone walkway to their house. "And I'll be sure to talk to the Council, too, though I don't know how much good it will do since even the Incorporation seems to be on the Outer Guard's side these days."

"Thanks, Mom." She turned to her mother, tears burning in her eyes. "Thank you for believing me and standing up for me, even if you think it won't work. I love you, Mom."

Lenora pulled her daughter into a tight hug. "I love you, too, Magnolia."

As soon as the words had left Lenora's mouth, the moment ended. The deep, tender feelings of a mother protecting her only child disappeared.

"Now that we're home, what can I do for you?" Lenora asked as Nola walked up the steps to the house.

"Nothing, Mom. But can you make sure my work team is up in the Amber Dome and ready in fifteen?"

"Of course." Lenora beamed up at her daughter. "It's always good to turn to your work, Nola. The seeds always make sense. And they will never hurt you."

Lenora turned and walked away without looking back.

Nola wanted to call after her and ask if that was why she preferred the company of seeds to her own daughter.

It won't matter soon.

The steps creaked under Nola's weight as she ran up them, pulling out her dresser drawer before she had even stopped moving. There was a narrow space at the back, discovered years ago when she and Kieran had needed a place to hide their childish secrets.

Carefully, she packed in vials, bottles, and packages, making sure there was no wasted room before sliding the drawer shut. From where she sat, there was no indication that she had done anything wrong. No blaring signals declaring Magnolia Kent had stolen from the domes once again.

What's next?

Nola crawled onto the bed, clutching the covers so her hands wouldn't shake. She needed a place to go and people to go with her. She knew enough about the outside world to be certain she would die quickly on her own. And she wouldn't leave T, Catlyn, or even Beauford in the domes. There was no bridge to the city anymore. No way for the domes to march them home when they were deemed no longer useful. She didn't want to imagine what the Council would do with them.

Moving to the bathroom in a daze, she stuck her head under the faucet of the sink and watched the red of the blood from her hair swirl down the drain. Her head stung as she pulled her hair into a tight braid. She needed to look normal, even if normal made her want to be sick again.

The walk to the Amber Dome seemed shorter than usual. Nola didn't read the signs that greeted her everyday as she normally did, even though they had been the same her whole life.

Her feet carried her to the Amber Dome without thought. She yanked on the brown gardening jumpsuit, not noticing what she had done until she pulled the zipper on the front all the way up.

People were already at work in the dome. The bloodshed of the night couldn't be allowed to affect the work of the day. There were more Domers working than there had been before, taking the place of Allory and the others who had attacked the guards the previous day.

"Miss Kent!" a voice called hesitantly from the far side of the dome. Catlyn gave a quick wave before dropping her hand and shrinking back into the bushes.

Nola ran over to her group, who were working on salvaging the bits of vine they had pushed through fleeing the fight.

"How are you?" Catlyn asked in a bright tone that sounded like she was merely being polite. But the intensity with which she stared at Nola told a different story.

"I'm fine." Nola smiled. "Doing well. Got a little bumped around on the bridge but nothing to worry about."

"You really were on the bridge?" T looked up from the vine she had been binding to a trellis. Her eyes were red and puffy as though she'd been crying.

"I was."

Catlyn gave a slow exhale through pinched lips. "We heard the guards talking and saw the bridge through the glass. I was hoping I had heard wrong."

"The bridge to the city was destroyed." Nola knelt down next to T, pointing at different parts of the vine without really looking at them. "There isn't a way for you to cross over the river to get home. There was a huge fire in the city last night, the biggest I've ever seen, and the Outer Guard aren't going to go back in to try and keep the peace. Now that we're cut off from the city, I don't know how bad things will get."

"Great," Beauford said from his place on the other side of the vines. "So even if we can get out of here and could find a way home, there won't be anything but wolves, Vampers, and death waiting for us. Glad you could give us that helpful information."

"I can't go back to the city." T shook her head, her face paling so her freckles were the only trace of color left. "How am I supposed to keep a baby safe with wolves running the streets?"

"Can you ask them to keep the baby?" Catlyn whispered, taking Nola's hands in hers. "There has to be a way to convince them. No one with a heart would send an innocent baby into a place where they have no chance of survival."

"The people of the domes don't have hearts," Nola said. She expected the words to hurt, to dig at something deep inside of her, but the void had swallowed the pain of that knowledge, too. "They will use you, then dump you outside. They probably won't even help you get across the river."

Fresh tears streamed down T's face.

"So we have to get out of here before they decide they're done with you. We have to break out of here and find Nightland." Nola ducked under the vines, feigning interest in the work Beauford had done. "You can't stay here, and after last night, neither can I."

"But you don't know where Nightland went," T said, leaning back down to the vines and attaching minuscule braces to the damaged section. "You swore you didn't."

"I don't know where Nightland is," she said, "but I know someone who does, or at least would know where to start looking."

"Can you trust them?" Beauford asked.

"I'll never trust her, but she needs my help if she wants to get out of her cell, and she's as close to Emanuel as we could hope to find."

"The Vamper in the cell," T said, then, seeing the shocked look on Nola's face, added, "I've heard the guards talking about her when they come into the hall."

"I'm sure she'd help us if I can get her out, and you out, and find a way out of the domes." Helplessness flared in Nola's chest.

"Getting out of the rooms only takes a code," Beauford said. "All you have to do is find out what it is. Getting out of the Guard barracks take a distraction."

"And getting out of the domes?" T asked.

"The domes are only made of glass."

CHAPTER TWENTY-THREE

"I need to see my work crew." Nola smiled sweetly at the Outer Guard who blocked the stairs to the barracks. "The ones who are in the cells in the back. It's my fault. I handed one of them a few seeds and asked her to keep them in her pocket while we worked. But I forgot to get them back, and now my mom, Lenora Kent, well, she's running inventory, and I really need to get those seeds back before she murders me."

The guard looked to his companion.

"I know I shouldn't have forgotten something so important, but with everything from last night..." Nola let her voice trail away for a moment, feeling foolishly dramatic. "I guess I'm just not thinking so well today."

"Fine," the guard finally said after a stiff nod from his partner, "but please don't tell anyone we let you in. And you've got to make it fast."

"I will." Nola sighed in relief as he led her through the barracks corridor. "I promise, I don't want anyone to know I made that sort of mistake. I mean, they aren't rare seeds. Just a few food plants, but my mother can be scary sometimes."

"I've heard rumors about Dr. Kent." The guard pushed open

the door to the hall of cells and stopped at the first one. "I don't blame you for wanting to stay on her good side. Even if she is your mother."

"Especially since she's my mother." Nola forced a laugh.

The guard tapped on the glass, drawing T, Catlyn, and Beauford's attention. They were all in the room together, just as Beauford said they had been last night.

"Catlyn," Nola called through the glass, "I forgot to get the seeds back from you."

"What, Miss Kent?" Catlyn shouted, looking toward the door. "I don't have any seeds."

The guard raised an eyebrow at Nola.

"Yes, you do," Nola said, her face now only a few inches from the glass. "I gave you the sealed dish to carry. But I never asked for it back."

"You did?" Catlyn patted her pockets a little more dramatically than necessary before pulling out the tray. "You're right! I'm so sorry, Miss Kent."

"It's not your fault. It's mine," Nola said. "But I do need to get it back tonight."

"Leave the dish on the floor and step away from the door." The guard stepped over to the numbered panel by the door.

"Thank you for helping me." Nola laid her hand on the guard's arm.

The texture of his uniform made her skin crawl, but she inched closer to him.

"Of course," the guard said. Pink rose in the guard's cheeks as he punched in the code.

25663

"Stand back." The guard opened the door and, in one swift movement, grabbed the dish of seeds and closed the door again. "And there you go."

"Thank you." Nola beamed. "Thank you so much. After last

night, I really don't think I could take any more stress. I'm not built for that kind of thing."

"I was there." Sympathy sounded in the guard's voice. "I saw you talking to that wolf, and you were great. But you can't always talk a crazy person out of doing a crazy thing."

"No, I guess not." They would be calling *her* crazy soon enough. "Is there any way I could talk to Captain Ridgeway while I'm down here? Just for a minute. After last night, I mean, well, I guess I don't understand everything that happened."

"Understanding what drugged-up outsiders do is impossible. I might have only been a guard for three years, but even I know that." He was young. Nola hadn't bothered to look before, but he was only a few years older than she was. And now Graylock had taken over his system.

Nola swallowed her scream. "I'd still like to try."

"We can see if he's in." The guard shrugged. "Just don't mention the seeds or me opening the door, all right?"

"Don't worry." Nola winked. "It'll be our secret."

The guard led her back out into the barracks corridor. There were still guards milling between rooms. It would have been better to come at night when everyone not on duty would be sleeping, but she needed the code.

The guard knocked on Captain Ridgeway's office door.

"Come in." Captain Ridgeway's rumbling voice sounded angry even through the thick metal.

"Are you sure you want to go in there?" The guard shrugged and swung the door open. "Miss Kent here to see you, sir." With a jerk of his head to the captain and Nola, the guard shut the door behind her.

"Nola." Captain Ridgeway stood behind his desk. She hadn't even started speaking, and his eyes had already narrowed suspiciously. "What can I do for you?"

"What happened to Lucifer and his pack?" she asked. "I know the story in the domes is that a pack tried to attack and blew themselves up. I've heard it repeated three times since lunch. But I know that isn't true. It wasn't one pack, it was a thousand people. And we blew up the bridge, not them."

Captain Ridgeway hesitated for a moment before tenting his fingers under his chin. "Fine, we blew up the bridge to cut off the domes from the city before the wolves could become a threat to our people. After what you saw last night, I would have assumed that would be self-explanatory."

"Is Lucifer dead?" Nola asked. "Did any of the Outer Guard see him in the fighting?"

"One thinks he fought him, but we didn't find a body. It's not unexpected. Between the fire and fighting so close to the broken ledge of the bridge, he could have been burned beyond recognition or fallen into the river."

"So, we just hope he's dead?" She wished the thought of Lucifer dead would bring at least a little sadness if for no other reason than the loss of precious life. But she had seen what he did to Allory, and she couldn't mourn a murderer. She could barely stand speaking to the one in front of her.

"We hope he's dead and hope even harder someone worse doesn't take his place." Captain Ridgeway sat back in his chair. "Of course, the city isn't our problem anymore. If they destroy themselves, so be it."

"And if they build boats and come for us again, will you burn the river to drive them away?" Nola's nails bit into her palms.

"I will burn the river and all of them with it. I believe in the mission of the domes with all that I am. And I will defend it with my life and with my children's lives. Don't forget what we're locked behind glass to do, Nola. We're here to save mankind, and if some have to be lost to let the human race survive, so be it."

"So be it." Nola nodded and turned for the door. She couldn't stand to look at him anymore.

"I'm glad you understand, Nola," Captain Ridgeway said.

She turned back around at the hardness of his tone.

"Jeremy seemed upset today," Captain Ridgeway said. "I won't pry into what goes on between the two of you. But you need to appreciate the sacrifices he is making for the domes. And for you."

She took a breath, begging the screaming in her head not to start again.

"I know Jeremy would do anything to protect me and the domes." She gave a pained smile and walked out of Captain Ridgeway's office, closing the door slowly behind her.

CHAPTER TWENTY-FOUR

The guards still stood at the end of the corridor, facing the stairs.

They were so trusting. Not even watching for the girl who had seen the code. Convinced of their safety behind glass walls.

Nola walked toward the hall of cells, not looking back to see if anyone followed.

Fingers trembling, she opened the door and stepped into the corridor. Closing it as silently as possible behind her, she turned and stared at the solid door to the Outer Guard's hallway.

"One, two, three," she counted. She couldn't afford to try unlocking the cells until she was sure she hadn't been followed. If she were caught, she would be banished without hope of taking the others with her or stealing any of the medicine she had hoarded in her room. "Ninety-seven, ninety-eight, ninety-nine, one hundred."

The door stayed shut. Nola walked to the door behind which T, Catlyn, and Beauford were trapped.

It only took a light tap on the glass for Catlyn to whisper, "Miss Kent."

25663

Nola held her breath as she punched in the numbers, only letting it out when the lock clicked open with a soft *beep*.

"Is everyone ready?" she whispered.

"Ready." Beauford was the first one out the door. He stood facing the exit to the Outer Guard barracks as the girls slipped past.

Nola ran down the hall until she reached the single cells. Raina lay on the floor of her cell just as she had the first time Nola had found her.

"Raina." Nola knocked on the glass.

Raina glanced up for only a moment before laying her head back on her arm.

"Raina, do you know where Emanuel is?" Nola asked.

"Torturing the filthy Vamper didn't work, so sending a lost little girl to ask questions will make me talk? Pathetic Domers," Raina grumbled, as though talking in her sleep.

"You don't have to tell me where he is," Nola said. "I only need to know if you can find him."

"I fought by Emanuel's side." Raina rolled onto her back and stared up at the ceiling. "I will always be able to find him."

"Will you take me to him?" Nola's heart crashed against her ribs. "Me and three outsiders the domes have trapped."

"Take you to him to kill him? To collect a bounty on his head? I'll take torture first." Raina curled back up into a tight ball.

"I'm leaving the domes," Nola said. "I can't stay here anymore. They used me to murder people. I can't live with that."

"Huh!" Raina laughed. "So, he was right all along. The beautiful girl locked in the domes with a heart big enough to want to save the poor ones left out to die."

"Right now, I just want to save the people I'm taking with me," Nola said, her face so close to the glass her breath fogged her view of Raina. "The city is falling, I don't think there's anywhere left we can survive but wherever Emanuel is."

"Not my problem," Raina said.

"One of the girls is pregnant," Nola said. "The baby's father is with Nightland. Raina, please."

"I can't help you." She turned her head just enough to be able to peer at Nola through the matted strands of scarlet and purple hair. "Even if I wanted to tell you, words alone couldn't help you find Emanuel."

"I don't want words. I'm taking you with me."

Raina pushed herself up to her elbows and glared at Nola.

"I'm going to get you out of here, but you have to help us get out of the domes and take us to Emanuel." Nola spoke as though each word were a dart, throwing them at Raina, making sure she had no choice but to understand.

"You want to let the monster out of its cage, ask it for a favor, and hope it doesn't rip your throat out?" Raina pushed herself to her shaky legs and wobbled to the door.

"You aren't a monster," Nola said. "You saved me when Nightland attacked. The knife that got you stuck in here was meant for me. So yes, I am going to let you out and hope we can get out of the glass and to Emanuel without the Domers or the wolves killing us."

"You left out vampires and zombies." Raina gave a grin that didn't reach her eyes. "Fine, better to die on the outside than in this damned room."

"But no killing in the domes." Nola's fingers hovered above the keypad. "I know they hurt you, but we're not going to cut innocent throats to get out of here."

"I think our definitions of innocent might differ," Raina said.

"No killing on the way out. Or I swear I will leave you in this cell to rot." Nola held Raina's gaze, every instinct telling her the vampire was searching her for a sign of weakness.

"Fine," Raina said after a long moment. "I won't kill anyone, unless they try to kill me first. Is that all right with you, oh mighty rescuer?"

"If they try and lock us back up, we'll all fight, Nola," Catlyn said. "We won't have a choice."

Nola scrunched her eyes closed, trying to block out the memories of the domes' floors smeared with blood.

"Fine."

25663

Panic seized Nola's heart for the split second between pressing the 3 and the *beep* of the door unlocking. Raina twisted the door handle and pushed it open, her legs wobbling as she stepped out into the hall. "And here I didn't think I'd ever get out of that cell."

"How are we going to get past the guards to the stairs?" T asked, the twisting of her fingers the only betrayal of her fear.

"*I'm* going to get past the guards by the stairs." Nola walked down the hall. "You wait until there's an opening and run for it. Don't let yourselves be seen. Raina will take you to where the way through the glass used to be. I'm sure she'll remember where it was. She used it before."

"Too right I did." Raina stumbled and tipped forward. Catlyn and Beauford both lunged to catch her before her face hit the ground.

"Is she going to be able to make it out of here?" T whispered to Nola.

"*She* can still hear you," Raina snarled as Catlyn helped her to her feet, "but *she* hasn't eaten in a month. Let's try starving you for that long and see how well you do?"

"They haven't fed you for a month?" Nola asked, louder than she'd meant to. She clapped a hand over her mouth, and the group waited in silence for a moment.

"I think they wanted to see if it would break me," Raina said. "Or maybe they just wanted to see how long a vampire lasts without a food source. Besides, I don't think they would have found it tasteful to feed a guest of the domes blood."

"You need to eat." T turned to Nola. "Do you have something sharp?"

"What? No."

T reached into Nola's pocket and pulled out the glass seed dish. She took off the top and passed the bottom that held the seeds back to her.

"T, don't," Nola began, but T had already placed the lid on the ground and stomped on it, breaking the glass with a crunch. Without pausing, she reached down and picked up the largest piece of glass, moving it toward her neck.

"T, no." Catlyn grabbed T's hand. "You can't do that with the baby. You need all the blood you have to stay healthy."

"She needs to eat, or we won't make it out of here," T said.

"Then use me," Catlyn said. "You make the cut, and she can drink from me. I'm not growing a human life. I'm sure I have blood to spare."

The two women stared at each other for a moment before T raised the piece of glass to Catlyn's neck, making a small cut right above her shoulder.

Ruby drops formed on Catlyn's skin, sparkling in the artificial light of the hall.

"Thank you," Raina breathed.

"Well, eat up," Catlyn said. "I can't stand here bleeding all night."

Raina licked the first drop of blood that rolled down Catlyn's pale flesh. The hall spun for a second, but Nola couldn't look away as Raina lowered her mouth over the wound and greedily began to drink. Catlyn turned her head away and froze, never moving as Raina drank.

A faint tinkling sound cut through the air as T dropped the bit of glass she had used to slice Catlyn's flesh. Her fingers were bleeding, but she didn't seem to mind. Blood couldn't bother her if she had sold her own to the Vampers of Nightland. Pale scars lined the base of T's neck. Nola had never noticed them before.

I didn't want to look.

"Thank you," Raina said a few minutes later as she pulled away from Catlyn. Blood coated her lips, but rather than making her look like a monster, it made her look glamourous. Like the blood was nothing more than shiny red lipstick.

"Are you sure you don't need more?" Catlyn pressed her sleeve to her neck. The wound had nearly stopped bleeding.

"We can't afford to slow you down either." Raina grinned, showing red-stained teeth.

"Right." Nola spun to face the door. "When the hall is clear, you get out of here. I'll meet you at the way out."

With more confidence than she felt, Nola pulled the door to the cell corridor open and walked out into the barracks corridor. The two guards still stood at the stairs with their backs to her. Faint voices sounded in the barracks, but there were no longer people meandering around the hall.

Keeping her shoulders back, Nola walked toward the stairs, not looking at the guards as she passed them.

"Everything all right then?" one of the guards called up after her. The young one she had spoken to before. He smiled up at her expectantly as though hoping she would stay and talk to him more.

"Everything's fine." She forced herself to smile. "Well, I suppose as fine as things ever get these days. And thank you, for everything."

Nola climbed the steps, ignoring the sounds of the second guard laughing at the first. They were deep down in the tunnels, laughing, secure in their safety. How could they forget fires and blood so quickly?

As soon as she was up the first flight of steps and out of sight of the guards, Nola turned and walked a few feet down the hall leading off in the opposite direction of Bright Dome.

Heart racing, she opened her mouth to scream. "Ahh. Ouch! Help! Can you please help!" She let her voice wobble as she lay down on the floor, hoping her cry had been enough to illicit action but not panic.

"Miss Kent!" the young guard called up the stairs. Two sets of heavy footsteps came running.

Both guards appeared at the top of the steps, weapons drawn.

"Miss Kent"—the young guard knelt next to her while the other's gaze swept the hall—"what happened? Have you been attacked?"

"No, I just"—Nola pushed herself halfway to sitting before falling back to the ground—"I was walking, and I got so dizzy. I fell, I think I hit my head."

"There weren't any intruders?" the second guard asked.

"No." Heat flooded Nola's cheeks. "I think I just panicked or something. I'm so sorry."

"We need to get you to the medical unit." The young guard moved to pick her up as the other turned back toward the stairs.

Not enough time.

"I can walk." Nola pushed herself to her feet, swayed, and toppled toward the guard who had been walking away.

"Careful!" the young guard shouted.

Nola clawed at the back of the other guard. He spun to face her, a look of fear on his face Nola felt sure he hadn't worn when fighting wolves.

Nothing more terrifying to a strong man than a fainting woman.

Nola hid her smile as she fell back to the floor, gasping for breath.

"I can't—" Nola wheezed. "I can't breathe!"

Both guards stared at her now.

"Please, I can't breathe!"

"Go get a doctor," the young guard said. The other turned to move, but Nola caught him by the front of his uniform, stopping him from turning just as four sets of feet crept by.

"No!" she said. "Home. Please, I want to go home."

"You need a doctor," the young guard said.

"No, I can't go see them again. Please." Nola pushed herself up to her elbows. "I've already been there today. I got hit on the head, and with the bridge..." Tears streamed from her eyes. "I really think I'm all right. I just want to go home."

"Are you sure?" The older guard stood and backed away.

"Really, thank you." Nola smiled wanly when the young guard helped her to her feet. "Please don't tell anyone about this. I don't think I can take being poked by a doctor again."

"Sure," the young guard said, easing his grip on her arm, "but if you keep not feeling your best, you might have to go see the doctor anyway. Don't let yourself get sick. Every citizen of the domes is needed, and needed healthy now more than ever."

Nola nodded and walked up the hallway, feeling their eyes on her. She wanted to rip her skin off, to get rid of every bit of flesh those guards had touched.

Needed healthy now more than ever. Breeding. He was talking about breeding.

Fighting the urge to run with every step, Nola walked up the corridor with a forced calm. She would have to go the long way around to Bright Dome. Stuck for even longer in the tunnels buried in the ground.

I'll never have to walk these tunnels ever again.

The thought stopped her in her tracks, the sheer weight of it locking her feet to the floor.

She was leaving her home. The only place she had ever lived. The place where she was born and learned to walk and talk. The place where her father had read to her at night, where she and Kieran had played in the trees. Where she had watched the gray smoke climb in the sky when her father died in a terrible riot in the city. Where she had watched them banish Kieran to the other side of the glass. Where she had let herself love Jeremy.

"I'm not abandoning the domes," Nola whispered to the empty hall. "The domes abandoned me."

Muscle memory brought her the rest of the way to Bright

Dome and up the stone walkway to her house. If she listened hard, she imagined she could hear faint rustlings and whispers under the willow tree, but it wasn't time for her to join the others yet.

The lights in the house were off. It wasn't surprising that Lenora wasn't home. Nola wished for a moment that she were. That she could hug her mother one last time. But it would have made leaving harder, so perhaps the dark house was better after all.

It only took her a few minutes to steal the backpack from under her mother's bed. To pull on the warmest clothes she had and shove a few changes into the bag on top of the vials. She managed to empty the kitchen cabinets and fill the three bottles she could find with water so quickly it hardly seemed like she was moving at all. Only the heavy weight of the pack on her shoulders made it seem real.

"Goodbye," Nola said to the empty house, then walked out the door.

CHAPTER TWENTY-FIVE

Nola stayed off the path as she made her way to the willow tree. Night had fallen, and it was easy to slip unseen through the darkness.

"It's me." Nola stepped around the bushes to the open patch of grass behind the willow tree. The tiny space was crowded with four people crouching in it.

"Took you long enough," Raina said.

"We thought you might have been caught." Catlyn gave Nola's hand a squeeze.

"We all could be if we stay here," Beauford said.

"You'll be grateful I took my time when you have something to eat in the morning." Nola knelt with the others. "Could you get the pane out?"

"Mostly," Raina said, lifting a thin metal bar in her hand, "but it didn't seem right to pull it the rest of the way free without you."

"Where did you get that?" Nola asked.

The thing Raina held looked like a weapon. And sparkling on her hip was a knife, attached to a pair of worn leather pants that matched her leather top.

"Sweet, sweet Nola," Raina said. "Never, ever invade an

enclosed environment without stashing a few backup supplies. I must say when I was slowly starving to death, I didn't think my extra bag of goodies was going to do me a damn bit of good, but what do you know? My hoarding paid off."

Raina kicked a bag with the tip of her toe. Dirt covered the canvas bag, as through it had been buried. T held up a small dagger and, now that she looked, Nola could see Catlyn and Beauford had weapons, too.

"Where did you bury them?" Nola reached for the bag. A narrow blade eight inches long was all that remained in the canvas sack.

"Outside your house, of course." Raina shrugged. "Now, if you've finished marveling at my brilliance and foresight, can we get to the escaping part of this escape?"

"Do it." There wasn't a trace of hesitation in Nola's voice.

Raina stood in the shadows and jammed the bar into the crack between the panes. It wasn't like when Doctor Wynne had pried the loose pane out with his fingers. The weakness Doctor Wynne had utilized had been sealed. But Raina was a vampire, and even the small bit of blood Catlyn had given her had brought back some of Raina's unnatural strength.

Nola held her breath, waiting for the pane of glass to move, but the glass wasn't sliding away. Thin lines formed in the pane, making a spider web just before the glass shattered with an ear-splitting *crack*. The sound rattled, echoing around the dome, but Raina didn't stop moving.

"Did you hear that?" a voice called on the other side of the trees.

"Is it the Vampers, Mommy?" a tiny voice asked, before the child started to howl.

Raina didn't pause to listen to the fear of the people who lived in Bright Dome. In seconds, there was another *crack* as the outer pane shattered.

"Go." Raina shoved T through the hole in the glass. Catlyn was out after her in a moment with Beauford close behind.

"You next," Raina whispered as voices drew closer.

"I'm not leaving you in here alone with children and a knife."

"Touché." Raina grinned and ducked through the glass.

"I think there's someone back there!" a voice shouted from not fifteen feet away. "Hello? Hello?"

"Someone call the guards!" a woman shrieked.

Nola dropped to her knees and crawled past the opening. Glass cut into her palms, but it didn't matter. In a few seconds, she was free.

A strong hand grabbed her under the arm, hoisting her to her feet. Nola bit back her scream as she saw Beauford steadying her, and they both ran down the hill, the other three following.

Raina quickly took the lead, tearing through the darkness at top speed.

Nola raced to catch up, her feet pounding against the ground.

She had found the way under the river once before, but it would take her time to do it on her own. They needed Raina if they wanted to beat the guards.

"T!" Catlyn shouted from behind.

Nola turned. T had fallen, panting, to the ground. She doubled back, wrapping her arm around one side of T's waist while Catlyn took the other.

"Keep running," Nola whispered. "We're going to find a safe place for your baby, but you have to keep running."

T swayed even while she ran but didn't stop moving.

A sharp wailing split the night as the domes' sirens blared.

Without speaking, Beauford dropped back to run behind the women, knife in hand. Nola wanted to tell him to run ahead with Raina, that a knife would do him no good against the Outer Guard's rifles, but she couldn't spare the breath.

The crisp, cool night air did nothing to help the burning in Nola's lungs. The shadows of the dead and dying trees looked like hands reaching out to grab them and drag them into some terrifying darkness. Every instinct told her to stop, to turn away from the shadows, but there was no time.

"The woods!" a voice shouted from up the hill. The Outer Guard had found them.

They reached the cover of the trees. Guns fired, breaking away chunks of wood that flew through the darkness, throwing the shadows into confusion. Raina ran ahead of them. Nola could only keep track of her by the shimmering of her hair in the pale light of the domes.

"Leave me," T panted. "They'll catch you. Please leave me."

"Not gonna happen." Beauford shoved Nola aside, lifting T in his arms and charging forward.

"This way." Nola took the lead, weaving through the trees as she followed Raina.

Shots cracked against the trees, but their trunks were too closely packed for the silver darts to find their marks. "Why are they firing at us?" Nola asked, her words coming out in gasps. "They can't hit us."

A string of sharp blasts sounded up ahead.

"They're corralling us," Catlyn said, running forward as fast as ever, a slight hunch of her shoulders the only sign that she knew the shots could hurt her.

They were getting close. With Bright Dome over to the left, they were nearly there. But they were too far back in the trees. They would need to run farther out to get to the way across the river.

"Come on." Nola ducked through the trees, barely making it in time to see Raina disappear into a shadow in the side of a tree.

Nola dived into the darkness, not stopping until she ran into a wall. She knew there were steps beneath her, but there was no way to see them.

Hands closed around her waist, lifting her over and down just as another person entered the darkness, panting. A faint grunt and thud told her Beauford and T had arrived.

"Slowly, down the steps," Raina whispered, so softly Nola could barely hear the words over her own breathing.

Nola reached her toe into the solid black, her hands stretched out in front of her, searching for a wall. She found one stair, and then another.

"Nola!"

Nola froze, teetering between steps.

"Nola!" Jeremy's voice ripped through the darkness. "Nola, where are you? Nola, please come out!"

He wasn't far away. She could hear him as though he were standing just beyond the tree.

Nola held her breath, waiting for lights to beam down on them and tiny silver needles to pierce their flesh.

"Raina, if you give Nola back to us unharmed, we will let you go. You can run off into the darkness and hide, and we won't ever come looking for you. But if you make her go with you, I will tear apart every piece of this planet to find her. When you sleep, I'll be hunting you. Where you feed, I will be tracking you."

There were shouts in the distance, men running the other way.

I hope they don't find a poor outsider.

"Nola," Jeremy called, his voice tighter than it had been before, "I know you're mad at me, at the domes. I know you think what we're doing is wrong, but it's not. You aren't one of them, Nola. Maybe they made you think you are, but you are a citizen of the domes. And whatever they have manipulated you into believing is a lie. I will fight to bring you home, Nola. With everything I have, I will fight for you. I love you, Magnolia Kent, and when you figure out everything they've been telling you is a lie, when you want to come home, I'll be here waiting. I promise."

Pain stabbed through her chest, puncturing the void that had protected her heart. He was shouting to the night that he loved her. That he would wait for her. But he didn't yet understand what she had done. And when he did...

He'll keep waiting for me.

Nola buried her face in her hands to muffle the sound of her tears. A cold hand took her elbow, leading her down the last few steps. A tiny scraping filled the darkness. It should have made her afraid, but she couldn't feel beyond the terrible pain in her chest.

The cold hand pulled her forward again, and the air changed, the chill tingle of outside air replaced by the stench of forgotten darkness.

Shuffling of feet and another faint scraping as the door shut behind them, then a *clink* as the door locked. It was done. Nola Kent had returned to Nightland.

CHAPTER TWENTY-SIX

"Can they get through the door?" Catlyn's whisper broke the silence.

"If they can find it," Raina murmured mere inches from of Nola's face.

Nola gasped and stepped backward onto a foot.

"Watch it," Beauford said.

"Sorry." Nola stretched her hands out in front of her, moving away from the group.

"Well, if they can get through the door, don't you think we should get out of"—Catlyn's voice faded for a moment—"wherever it is we are?"

"It won't be easy in the dark. But hey"—Nola could hear the smile in Raina's voice—"who better to lead you through the dark than a creature of the night?"

"Comforting," Nola whispered.

"Take my hand, and follow the leader." Raina's cold fingers closed around Nola's wrist. She wanted to shout at Raina not to touch her, but she needed Raina to lead them.

A warm hand found Nola's other arm and moved down to take her hand.

"Catlyn?" Nola asked.

"It's me, Miss Kent," Catlyn said.

"Let me down, Beauford," T said from behind. "We aren't running now. I've caught my breath. I can walk on my own."

"Are you sure?" Catlyn asked.

"Positive," T said.

After a rustle of movement, Beauford said, "Ready back here."

"Look, an adventure in Nightland, how novel," Raina purred from the front. "You know, I really didn't think I'd ever come back here. It's not as homey without lights."

"Are we in Nightland?" Catlyn spoke just loudly enough for her voice to carry to Raina.

It hadn't occurred to Nola that the others wouldn't know where they were. She had told them she knew a way under the river. But she hadn't told them how. She was too afraid that, were they given the information, they would leave her behind. Or worse, turn her in. They had slipped through a hidden shadow in a dead tree, and now they were in the dark. Gratitude swelled in her chest, and she squeezed Catlyn's hand. They had trusted her with their lives.

"We are in Nightland," Nola said. "At least a tunnel that leads to the main part under the city. This tunnel will take us under the river to the place where all the vampires used to live."

"Magnolia Kent, tour guide of darkness," Raina snorted.

"I never knew there was a tunnel to the other side of the river," T said. Her voice sounded shaky, but they didn't have time to stop and let her rest.

"It wasn't something Emanuel liked to advertise," Raina said. "Only a handful of people knew about the way to get to the domes. Hundreds of hungry, angry vampires living packed together, and you tell them it's only a short walk to make a meal out of the people they hate? Emanuel didn't think most would be able to resist the temptation. He didn't tell the masses until it was time to attack."

"Massacre," Nola said without anger in her voice. "It wasn't an attack. It was a massacre done by thieves. You weren't just killing guards."

"If you think that was a massacre, you clearly need to spend more time on the streets," Raina said. "Out here we call that a Thursday night."

A low laugh sounded from the back of the group.

"Oh, the big guy thinks I'm funny," Raina said.

"It's Beauford."

"Hmmm." Raina didn't say anything else as the tunnel sloped downward.

Nola shut her eyes against the darkness, trying not to think about the thick layers of dirt looming over her. But the air wasn't freshly filtered here like it was in the tunnels of the domes. The stench was enough to tell her the river above could kill them if it chose to.

"How did you even dig this?" Catlyn asked, as though reading Nola's mind for the question she hadn't wanted answered.

"A few old geologists and a lot of muscle. A few people dying, too, of course, but these things happen." Raina's words turned Nola's spine to jelly.

Each step became harder as her body decided on her behalf that there was no point in walking any farther. That the tunnel was just going to cave in and kill them anyway.

But Raina kept pulling her forward, keeping a steady pace, never seeming to doubt which way her feet should be going.

Then the tunnel angled upward.

"When we get to the other side of the tunnel door, there might be some people around," Raina said. "Try not to get killed or lost. I'm not going to waste my time running around Nightland searching for lost lambs."

"We just have to get through Nightland to the street," Nola said. "Once we get up there, you can take us to Emanuel."

"Absolutely." Raina's pace slowed. "I just have to run one little errand first."

"Errand?" T asked.

"It's only a little out of the way. And besides, you can't go anywhere without me." Raina stopped suddenly, and Nola rammed into her back.

"Fine," Nola said, "but make it quick. If the Outer Guard find the tunnel and figure out where we are, we won't be able to get to the street. Then we'll never find Emanuel."

"Quick as a genetically-modified bunny." Raina let go of Nola's hand.

The high screech of metal grinding against stone cut through the darkness. The air changed again as Raina led them forward. The dampness lessened, replaced by the stench of filth and stale blood.

"This way." Raina took her hand again, pulling her through the pitch black.

Nola knew where they were now. In the main body of Nightland, where tunnels split off in every direction. There were dozens of halls and hundreds of doors.

"Will you be able to find your way in the dark?" Nola asked as the door scraped shut behind them.

"Do you have a flashlight you've been hiding?" Raina said.

"No."

"Well then, I guess I'll have to find my way in the scary dark," Raina said. "Try not to ask stupid questions while I'm concentrating."

Nola bit her lips together and followed obediently. She hadn't packed a flashlight. It hadn't even occurred to her while she tossed what she thought she would need for the outside world into a bag.

What else did I forget?

"There used to be electricity down here," T said. "In all the tunnels I ever saw. More electricity than we had in the houses aboveground. I wonder why it stopped running."

"No one to keep it going?" Catlyn said.

"Or the guards cut it off," Beauford said.

"Not all of it," Nola said, squinting as far up the tunnel as she could see. A dim light glowed in the distance, flickering like some kind of flame.

"Well, shit," Raina said.

"Wha—" Before Nola could fully form the word, a shout sounded from the back of the group.

"Beauford!" Catlyn screamed.

But thudding and grunting were the only response.

"Dammit." Raina let go of Nola's hand and a *swish* sounded, like a knife clearing its sheath.

Someone screamed, but Nola couldn't tell who. Her hand fumbled for the knife in her waistband. Before she could find it, something had grabbed the back of her pack and thrown her against the wall.

"Don't touch me!" T screamed. "I am carrying a child of Nightland!"

Her words made the sounds of the fight change but didn't stop a hand from closing over Nola's mouth and wrenching her head sideways. She kicked back as hard as she could, sinking her teeth into the hand that held her.

The sickening taste of blood filled her mouth, but the person holding her only laughed. With a twist of her arm, she pulled her knife free and plunged it behind her. The thin blade cut into flesh, but the one holding her kept laughing. A high, maniacal laugh accompanied by warm breath that touched her neck and crawled across her skin.

Nola pulled the knife back out and stabbed again, and again. On the sixth stab, she managed to hit higher than before, and the one who held her finally seemed to register the pain. With a howl, he pushed her away. She flew sideways, tripping over something that lay on the ground before hitting the opposite wall. Her knife slipped out of her hand. In the darkness, not even a faint shimmer of metal told her where it might have landed.

"You pricked me!" a low voice growled.

Nola dropped to her knees, feeling frantically around in the dirt. A person lay on the floor, warm blood pooling around them, but Nola didn't have time to wonder who the person might be. Her fingers found something hard as a hand closed around her neck.

"What makes you think you can stab me?" the voice shouted, at the same time another voice that sounded horribly like Catlyn's screamed.

Nola grasped the metal thing as she was lifted into the air by her neck. The sharp blade of the knife cut into her palm. She wanted to drop it, to make the shooting pain stop, to claw away the hand that choked her so easily.

But she grabbed the hilt of the knife with her other hand and swung it down toward the arm that held her. The blade cut deep into the man's flesh, the force of it nearly pulling the knife from her grip. The fingers loosened, and she crumpled to the ground, but she didn't drop the knife this time. She dove into the darkness and stabbed. The man bellowed in pain as she sank her knife into every part of him she could find.

A scream tore from her throat, but she didn't know how to make the noise stop. The only thing she could think was to kill the man. Kill the Vamper so his hand couldn't close around her throat again. She couldn't see where his heart would be, so she knelt and stabbed again and again. Cold hands closed around her wrists.

"I've got it." Raina lifted Nola off the man's chest. "Give me some space. It's not easy decapitating someone in the dark with a knife."

Nola sat back on the ground. Both of her hands touched blood. She was surrounded by it, a sea of unseeable red.

"Is everyone okay?" Nola's voice wavered.

"I'm fine," T said from farther down the hall.

"One of the Vampers bit me," Beauford said. "But I'll live."

"I think," Catlyn wheezed from right behind Nola, "I think I might not."

CHAPTER TWENTY-SEVEN

"What?" T said. Footsteps sounded as she came closer.

"What happened?" Nola felt her way toward Catlyn's voice, climbing over a body in the darkness. "Where are you hurt?"

"Too many places, Miss Kent." Catlyn coughed a laugh. "I don't know which bits are bleeding worst."

"Catlyn, you're going to be all right." Beauford's hands brushed past Nola, reaching for Catlyn. A sharp intake of breath told Nola what he felt wasn't good. "We need Vamp. Raina, we need Vamp."

"Give her to me," Raina said, moving past Nola who felt Catlyn's body rise as Raina lifted her. "I know where there'll be some."

"No Vamp," Catlyn said. "If you can't save me, don't give me Vamp. I won't live without the sun."

"We have ReVamp." Raina ran down the hall.

Nola took off after them, charging toward the distant flickering light.

"ReVamp is different," Raina said, not showing any signs of being out of breath, despite carrying a full-grown woman while she ran. "You'll still be you. No personality changes, no violent urges. You'll have to deal with drinking blood and living in the dark, but it's a hell of a lot better than death."

"Not for me," Catlyn croaked.

"Then we'll help you without Vamp or ReVamp," T said. "We'll clean the wounds and bandage you up and you'll be just fine."

"You know better than that, T," Catlyn murmured.

"I won't give up on you."

They reached the light just in time for Nola to see tears streaming down T's face as they ran.

Nola glanced back at Beauford. He ran slower than the rest, barely keeping up as he tried to stop the blood that flowed from a bite mark on his arm.

Torches lined the halls here. The torches hadn't been there when Nola had walked the corridors with Kieran. Someone had left them. People were living in Nightland again.

We can't survive more Vampers.

"Catlyn!" T shouted as Catlyn's eyes drifted shut. "Catlyn!"

But Catlyn didn't open her eyes, and her head bounced with each step Raina took.

"Who's down there?" a voice called from around a corner.

Raina dodged into a side hall and kept running. The electric lights were still working in this corridor though half of the bulbs had shattered.

"Where is the Vamp?" Beauford asked.

"I don't know if we're going to be able to get into Emanuel's house," Nola said. "If there are people living down here, I don't know a place more appealing than Emanuel's."

"That's not where the ReVamp is." Raina turned another corner, ducking into a side passage when the sounds of boisterous laughter carried to them from up ahead.

"She needs it now," Beauford said. His steps had grown uneven, and blood dripped from his fingertips. If it got much worse, Catlyn wouldn't be the only one who needed a dose of ReVamp.

They turned into a narrow corridor. The few doors that lined the walls hung loosely from their hinges. Dark stains coated the ground. Chunks of the stone wall had been knocked free.

Raina slowed to a walk.

"We don't have time for this." Beauford moved past Nola to Raina.

"We're here." Raina laid Catlyn on the ground.

The weight of all the earth above them crashed down into Nola's stomach.

A ragged bite marked Catlyn's neck, a deep wound on her shoulder looked like nails had ripped her flesh away, and a gash that reached from her ribs to her stomach left her entire torso drenched in blood.

Crack.

Raina kicked the wall five feet away from Catlyn.

Crack.

Dust and rocks fell to the ground.

"Please don't." T stepped forward, but Raina kicked the wall again.

Crack!

A two-foot square of wall crumbled away.

Blowing the hair out of her eyes, Raina reached into the wall and pulled out a dust-covered, silver case.

"Out of the way," Raina said, but T didn't step aside.

"Move!" Raina growled, opening the box and pulling out a needle.

"I can't." T's voice sounded like she had been ill for months.

"Do not make me be the bad guy who throws a pregnant girl against a wall."

"I can't let you give her that shot." T raised her chin, staring defiantly at Raina.

"You can't let me save your friend's life?" Raina shook her head and moved to sidestep T, but T blocked her path again.

"She doesn't want the drugs." Tears streamed down T's face. "Not Vamp or ReVamp, not Lycan or anything else. She doesn't want it."

"I doubt she wants to die either," Raina spat. "Take it from someone who just kicked a hole through a stone wall without breaking a sweat. Drinking a little blood is way more fun than dying."

"Not for her," T whispered. "Catlyn has lived a long, hard life. Who are we to take her death from her? She said she would rather die. If that's what she wants, then we have to let her go."

"Let her go? Let her go!" Raina laughed. "And where do you think she'll be going? We certainly won't be able to bury her. We could leave her here in case a wolf gets hungry. If they don't want her, I'm sure the bugs and the rats will have a fine feast."

"Stop." Nola leaned against the wall.

"And where will she be when there's nothing left but bones and rot?" Raina stepped so close to T their faces were nearly touching. "She doesn't want to live in the darkness? Darkness is all that waits for her as she decays into nothing."

"Stop it!" Nola's scream echoed against the walls. "Catlyn didn't want to be a vampire. She wanted to die, so let her do it. She died escaping the domes, let that be her end."

"How poetic." Raina held the needle in her hand up to the dim light. A faint, shimmering liquid, so thin it could barely be seen, filled the needle. In a practiced motion, she rolled up her sleeve and shoved the needle into her vein, sighing as she pressed the serum into her blood. "Fine, more ReVamp for me." She looked at Nola, her eyes shining a darker black than they had a moment before. "Or anyone else who actually wants to survive to see Emanuel." She tossed the needle against the wall, and it clattered to the ground with a finality that shook Nola more than the hand around her throat had.

"Catlyn." T knelt down next to her.

Catlyn didn't look like she was breathing.

She might already be dead.

"Thank you." T pressed Catlyn's bloody hand to her lips. "Thank you for taking care of a lost girl. Rest well, my friend, and never know pain again." She laid Catlyn's hand on her torn stomach and stood. "We should go."

"Is she dead?" Beauford asked.

"Close enough." T wiped her hands on her pants, but it didn't take away the bloodstains. "We have to go. Catlyn wouldn't want us to risk ourselves to watch her die."

"She'll never *want* anything again," Raina said.

"How do we get out of here?" Nola asked. If they were going to leave Catlyn lying in a hall, it was better to do it quickly before the evilness of abandonment set in.

"There's a back way." Raina relocked the silver case. "It'll be easier to get to but nasty once we hit open air."

"Will there be a place for daylight?" T asked. "We can't have much longer until sunrise."

"I know a place," Raina said. "If we're lucky, I won't even have to kill anyone to get us in."

CHAPTER TWENTY-EIGHT

Raina led them farther down the hall where the ReVamp had been hidden, moving past more broken doors and shattered light bulbs.

"In here." Raina lead them through one of the dingiest-looking doors.

Someone had scrawled words onto it. A long string of something Nola didn't take the time to read.

The room was so small, the light from the hall lit the four cracked walls. Not pausing, Raina headed to a tiny closet in the back. Fabric had been tacked to the wall. Raina pulled it aside, revealing a tiny trap door.

"Big guy might have some trouble." Raina knelt and yanked a wooden panel out of the wall. "Anyone who minds a tight squeeze can feel free to head out the front."

"You first," Nola said.

Please let it be caved in.

It was an irrational thought. They needed to get out of Night-land before they were attacked again. They couldn't risk another fight. Not after Catlyn.

Nola's chest tightened. Grief and panic flooded her.

Raina slithered into the hole. In few seconds, all that showed were her feet.

"Come on in," Raina said. "Nothing here but a little vampire."

"I'll go." T knelt next to the hole.

For a moment, Nola was afraid her stomach wouldn't fit, but with little more struggle than Raina, she disappeared.

"You next," Beauford said.

"I can go last." Nola shook her head. She needed a minute, just one more minute outside the terrifyingly small space.

"I'm going last, and I'm not going to argue with you. Get in the damn hole."

Nola nodded, not trusting her voice to work, and knelt outside the tunnel.

A creaking sounded behind her. She spun to see Beauford closing the door. Everything melted into black.

"We can't afford to be followed," Beauford whispered over the sound of footsteps coming toward her.

"Right." Nola reached her hands out in front of her, feeling the edges of the tunnel. Her backpack was too big to fit through the gap on her back. She would have to push it in front of her.

For how long?

She closed her eyes and slipped off her pack, pushing it into the tunnel.

"A little faster if you don't want us to die," Beauford whispered.

Lying down on her stomach, Nola slid into the tunnel. Dragging herself forward with her hands, she moved a few feet before pushing up onto her hands and knees. The ceiling touched the back of her jacket, but she could still move forward. Push the backpack, move forward a foot. Push the backpack, move forward a foot.

"Nola, Beauford?" T said, from what seemed like miles in front of Nola. "Are you coming?"

Yes. Nola thought the word, but it didn't make any sound. "Yes."

"It gets a little tighter up here. Make sure you watch your head."

Tighter. The tunnel got tighter.

She dug her nails into the dirt and stone beneath her.

Catlyn was right to want to die in Nightland. It was better than dying trapped in a tunnel.

Nola's breathing quickened as the blackness around her spun.

"Are you all right?" Beauford said. "Miss Kent, are you okay?"

"I-I c-can't move," she whimpered, fighting for each bit of air she pulled into her lungs. "There's no air. I can't breathe."

"You can breathe. There's air just in front of you. Move ahead, and there'll be air."

Nola didn't think her arms were capable of moving, but Beauford's words made sense. There had to be air somewhere. It couldn't have all disappeared at once.

"Just move up a foot, and there'll be air," Beauford said.

Shaking, she pushed the backpack a foot ahead and crawled after it.

"See, it's better already, isn't it?" Beauford's voice sounded closer now. "Think how good it will be in another foot. Go on. Try one more foot."

The air didn't feel better. It was thick and stale, too fleeting for her lungs to grasp.

But Beauford sounded so sure. "You're nearly to the open air now. If you move just another foot, you'll be able to smell it. Just one more foot."

Nola nodded in the darkness. One more foot. One more foot, and she could breathe.

The process went on and on. Beauford urging her to move, Nola fighting for every inch she gained.

"Nola." The darkness changed as the backpack was pulled out of Nola's path. Shadows replaced the thick pitch black.

A cold hand grabbed her wrist and dragged her out of the tunnel and onto a wooden floor.

"I thought you might have died in there," Raina said, without a trace of concern in her voice.

Nola rolled onto her back, panting.

The air here smelled thick with dust and the scent of decay she had only ever smelled in the woods.

"Is she all right?" Beauford asked.

"I'm…" Nola began but couldn't spare the breath to finish saying she was fine now that there was air.

"I think the Domer might be a little claustrophobic. Funny being afraid of small spaces when there are monsters in the world," Raina said.

"I know there are monsters." Nola sat up, regretting it as her head spun. "But being trapped in the dark with no air feels worse. You can't fight air."

"How…literal." Raina pulled back the thick curtains that covered the window, letting faint light into the dismal room.

The wooden floor was worn, warped, and dirty. Dust coated the peeling wallpaper, which looked far older than Nola. A chair had been broken apart and tossed by the filthy fireplace that showed no signs of having been recently lit.

"Where are we?" Nola stood.

Beauford took her elbow to steady her. "Careful, Miss Kent."

"Nola. Please call me Nola."

"Nola," Beauford said. "Be careful."

"Fantastic." Raina grinned sarcastically. "If we're finished, we should probably get to a safe place before dawn."

"This isn't the safe place?" Nola said.

"You're never safe near the escape. It's too easy to be found." Raina rolled her dark eyes as though Nola were the biggest idiot she had ever met. "What we need to do is disappear into the vastness of the city. The Outer Guard might be able to follow us through the tunnels, but they'll have one hell of a time following us through the streets."

"They'll tear the city apart to find us." Nola picked up the pack and settled it on her back. The weight of it seemed to have doubled while they were in the tunnel.

"I'm sure they will." Raina shrugged. "But it'll take time. And the farther we get from here, the longer it will take them. With any luck, by this time tomorrow night we'll be outside the city and on our way to Emanuel."

"Then let's get going." Beauford headed toward the one door in the room. His own blood coated his arm from the vampire bite.

"Wait." Nola slid the pack off her back. "You need medicine for your arm."

"Later." Beauford shook his head. "When we're safe. I'll survive until then."

"Smart man." Raina pushed past him and opened the door. "Try and stay close. You'll all be scented in a minute, and I really don't feel like fighting a bunch of wolves before dawn." She walked out into the hall. Beauford followed, but T stood behind Nola, carefully rolling up her shirt to show her swollen belly.

"You should go next," T said. "It'll be safer with me in the back."

"Why?" Nola asked. The floor squeaked as she walked across it, every step shouting to the world where they were.

"I know the outside must seem dark and lawless to you," T said, following Nola into the hall, "but there are some rules almost everyone will follow. I'm pregnant. Only the worst wolves would hurt me."

"Because you're carrying a vampire's baby? If you were carrying a werewolf's baby, would only the worst vampires hurt you?"

"Basically," T whispered her answer.

Closed doors lined the derelict hall. The smell of stale food permeated the air, and people spoke angrily behind one of the doors.

Nola took a few quick steps to catch up to Beauford, shoving aside the terrible feeling someone could pop out and grab her at any moment.

A big, wooden door blocked the end of the hall.

She tapped Beauford on the good arm and whispered softly, "What is this place?"

"An apartment building," Raina answered from the front in a carrying, conversational tone. "I'm sure you've never seen one. But out here a lot of people consider themselves lucky to live in a place this nice. Solid walls, sturdy doors. I think there's even running water in this one."

The door at the end of the hall burst open. Five men came in, laughing and staggering. One of them fell face-first onto the ground as he tried to cross the threshold.

"Ah, company!" the man at the front of the pack shouted, holding his arms out wide. "Look, boys, the party isn't over after all!"

"Yes, it is." Raina rested her hand on the hilt of her knife.

"The kitten has teeth!" one of the other men laughed.

"This *tigress* has fangs." Raina stalked toward the men. "And she likes to bite. She even likes blood. Anyone here want to give me a snack?"

"Don't be angry," the first man said, taking a step back and stumbling over his friend who still lay on the floor.

"Watch yourself!" the man on the ground shouted.

"I was only playing." Fear filled the first man's face. "I didn't mean anything by it. You be on your way and enjoy the rest of your night."

Raina backed the man into the wall. "Oh, we'll go." She leaned in so her cheek rested on his. "But what if I hadn't been a vampire? What if the kitty you wanted to play with hadn't had claws? What if I had been a poor defenseless little girl lost in the night?"

"I-I don't—"

"Sure you do," Raina cooed. "You would have taken me into the shadows whether I liked it or not."

She pulled her blade from its sheath and pressed the tip to the man's forehead without looking at her hand.

The man moaned in pain, but his friends did nothing.

"Next time, think before you decide someone is your prey, little pig. You'd make an excellent meal." She stepped back, lifting the blade to her mouth and licking away the single drop of blood that clung to its tip. "And now you're on the menu. Avoid dark hallways, little pig."

Kissing the man on the cheek, Raina turned and walked out the door.

She'd carved *V* into the man's forehead. The mark dripped blood down his nose and into his eyes.

"Come on." T strode through the men, and Nola followed, nearly stepping on T's heels as she escaped the hallway.

The sky was still dark, the faint moonlight leaving the streets as terrifying as the hallway had been. Raina led them down a long row of apartment buildings much like the one they had just left. Most were at least five stories tall, and each was broken down and sad in its own way. One missing a front door. Another with all the widows at the ground level shattered. Another had *Night Filth* scrawled across its bricks in bright red paint.

"You didn't have to do that to him," T said as soon as she caught up to Raina.

Walking behind them, a terrifying loneliness clawed at Nola's stomach until Beauford took his place next to her.

"She was right to do it," Beauford said.

"See, the big one agrees with me," Raina said, no hint in her voice that she actually cared what any of them thought.

"It's only a cut," Nola said. "I'm sure he'll heal."

"It's a v-shaped cut right on his face," T spoke through clenched teeth. "She just marked him as a meal. If he keeps showing his face outside at night, he'll be lucky to survive the week."

"Don't think of it as my limiting the time frame of his disgusting little life. Think of it as my giving him an opportunity to realize the error of his ways and have time to seek atonement in this cruel world."

Raina rounded a corner and headed down a street where the sidewalks had been piled high with trash. The sign on the corner read *Maggot Row*, and Nola didn't have to question where the street had gotten its name.

Raina moved to the very center of the street where a three-foot-wide path cut between mounds of rotting garbage.

The smell of decay hit Nola so hard, bile gurgled into her throat, but Raina and T kept moving forward, arguing about the man. Nola covered her nose with the collar of her jacket and tried to keep from wondering what had created the sticky squish under her feet.

"You condemned that man," T said. "He is going to die because you cut him."

"So I should have killed him in the hall?" Raina rounded on T, blocking the way forward.

Nola shook as the piles of trash seemed to creep closer and closer.

"Or should I have stepped aside and let those monsters do whatever they wanted to Nola? Hell, even big boy might have had a moment to shine with the cretins."

"That's not what—" T argued.

"Then I should have made them walk nicely away and let them find another girl who doesn't have a vampire with a knife trying to keep her alive and see what they do to her? There are far worse monsters in this world than I will ever be, little girl. Don't blame me for getting rid of one." Raina turned and walked through the alley between trash, not bothering to check if any of them followed.

"She doesn't understand," T began, but Beauford cut her off.

"She understands perfectly. You of all people should appreciate that. Now move before someone else comes along and Raina ends up killing them more quickly."

T opened and closed her mouth several times before biting her lips together and stepping carefully behind Nola and Beauford, waving a hand to tell them to move.

"Do you really think those men would have hurt us?" Nola asked as she and Beauford jogged after Raina.

"Yes." Beauford's single, apathetic word sent a shiver down Nola's spine.

She had chosen the outside, left everything she had to join it, to help save the humans in a monstrous world. It had never occurred to her that humans could be the ones she would need saving from.

CHAPTER TWENTY-NINE

They didn't speak as Raina led them through the city. The rows of trash finally ended, leaving them on a street that looked like it had recently seen a battle. The outsides of the buildings here were dented and cracked, like a hundred Rainas had decided they hated the bricks for existing.

No one was in sight, but Nola could sense people waiting just out of view. In the shadows behind rusted and burned out old cars. Lurking in the wooden crates that leaned against the buildings, their fronts covered in cloth as though hiding a sleeping person within.

Raina never paused, leading them down a street that had been taken by fire. The lopsided skeletons of the buildings were completely covered in black ash, but people slept within the ruins, huddled in thin blankets against the cold.

Raina turned onto a street unlike any of the others. A long row of houses with streetlights keeping the shadows at bay. There were no signs of fighting or fires here. The fronts of these buildings were well tended, and the only scent in the air was the perpetual stench of decay that was impossible to avoid in the city.

Six men appeared from the shadows as they approached.

"Stay right there," the first man said. He was tall and broad with a bat resting over his shoulder.

"Oh really?" Raina sauntered forward. "And I suppose you're going to make me?"

"Ma'am, this is a private street." The man with the bat stepped in front of Raina. "We can't have any trespassers."

"You must be new," Raina said. "My name is Raina, and if you want to keep your blood in your pathetic little veins, I suggest you step aside and apologize at once."

The man swallowed hard, his gaze traveling from Raina's black eyes to her scarlet-and-purple streaked hair, finally landing on her knife in its sheath.

"I apologize, Miss Raina." The man bowed deeply, keeping his eyes continually on the knife. "I was told you were dead."

"Death can be so hard to define these days," Raina said. "If you scamper like a good little guard and don't bother me again, I'll let you live. How's that?"

"Yes, Miss Raina." The man bowed again, backing away. "Thank you, Miss Raina."

The other guards followed, never taking their eyes off Raina as they disappeared into the shadows.

"They are adorable." Raina sighed. "Little, naïve things who think they can keep away the boogeymen."

"Who are they?" Nola whispered as they moved down the street. The windows in the buildings were dim, but the streetlights glinted off delicate curtains and plants resting on windowsills. "What is this place?"

"The guards were guards," Raina said, "and this is what we on the outside call a nice neighborhood. When the world falls apart, it doesn't happen all at the same rate. The people who live here own the factories that supplied the domes, are a part of the vague thing we like to call city government, or are just plain rich enough to pretend the city they live in isn't rapidly burning to the ground."

"It's pretty." Nola smiled as they passed a house with a bright blue door. "How many other places are there like this?"

"None," Beauford said. "Not anymore. There used to be a few streets like this."

"But Bellevue is the last one left." Raina ran up the stairs to a house and banged on the door. "Every time something horrible happened, another one of the nice streets would disappear. They'd rot gradually or burn magnificently, but either way they'd be gone. This is the last façade in the dying city."

Lights flicked on in the windows that flanked the door. A silhouette appeared, holding what looked like a handgun.

"Whoever you are, you had better get the hell off my steps and go back to wherever you came from!" a female voice shouted from inside the house.

"Tsk, tsk." Raina leaned into the crack by the doorjamb. "You really shouldn't swear like that. It's completely unbecoming of a lady."

The door swung open.

"You?" The woman from inside stepped toward Raina, pointing a gun directly into her face. "What are you doing here?"

"Is this any way to begin a homecoming?" Raina asked.

"I told you never to come back here." The woman stepped closer to Raina. She looked to be in her mid-fifties. Gray mixed in with her long, dark hair, and fine lines surrounded her full lips. "I told you, you don't belong here."

"I would take you at your word, but the guards backed away so nicely when I told them I'd come to pay a call on my baby sister," Raina said.

"I can call them over here right now," the woman said. "I won't let you bring your fighting and blood into this house."

"We aren't looking for a fight." T stepped forward. She moved with her bare belly pushed out, making her pregnancy more obvious than ever. "There are some bad people who are looking for us, and all we want is a place to sleep out of their way until we can leave. We only need a place for one day."

"You bring a pregnant girl to my house with some blood-covered tramps and expect me to have sympathy for any of you? Gah." The woman swung the door to the house fully open and stepped aside to let them in. "I want to know exactly what fresh hell you have brought to my door, Raina."

"*Our* door, little sister," Raina said as she shut and locked the door behind her. "Remember, sweet mommy and daddy left the place to both of us."

"You really are sisters?" Nola looked from one to the other.

"Of course Nettie and I are sisters." Raina pinched Nettie's cheeks.

"My name is not *Nettie*," Nettie growled.

"Call her Nettie." Raina smirked.

"I don't care what you tell the bloody little girl to call me, but please tell me why you're in my house and—"

"Our house."

"—who the hell is after you," Nettie finished.

"Language, little sister," Raina warned, locking eyes with Nettie in a glare neither of them seemed willing to break.

"The domes' Outer Guard," Nola finally said. "They were holding Raina and the other three..." Nola's voice trailed away. "The other two captive. They found out we escaped, and now they're looking for us."

"Captured by the domes?" Nettie raised a dark eyebrow. "Impressive even for you. But you didn't say where you"—she pointed her gun at Nola—"little bloody girl, come into play."

"She's a Domer," Raina said. "A Domer with a heart of gold who just had to save us poor outsiders locked in cells. Or you could say she's the infamous Nola Kent and has seen too much of the world to pretend it doesn't exist. Too bad poor *bloody girl* doesn't have a better imagination. She could be sleeping in her own bed right now."

"For God's sake, Raina, don't be rude to the infamous Nola Kent. If rumors are true, it's your lot's fault the city's going to shit more quickly than ever."

"Why thank you." Raina bowed.

"And thank you for bringing fugitives into my—"

"Our."

"—house," Nettie spat. "The last thing I need is a load of Outer Guard busting down my front door."

"You really hate that this is my house, too." Raina walked down the hall and rounded a corner. "Come on, you lot, enjoy *my* lavish living room."

"Fine, go," Nettie said, "but please don't get any blood or muck on the upholstery. It's nigh on impossible to replace these days."

"Still keeping up appearances as the world crumbles?" Raina lay sprawled out on a bright red couch in the center of the room, facing a fireplace that took up most of one wall. In one corner of the room sat a marble table, supporting a vase filled with silk flowers, while in another, a matching table held a sparkling decanter filled with amber liquid.

"I like to take good care of my things." Nettie stalked to the corner and poured herself a glass from the crystal decanter. The strong scent of liquor wafted across the room. "And get your feet off the couch."

Raina hesitated before lowering her feet to the floor. "Only because you're being so sweet to our guests."

"Anyone who is mixed up with you will need as much help as they can possibly get." Nettie held her glass in the air before taking a long drink. "The sun should be up in an hour or so. How many can't stand the sunlight?"

"Only me, baby Nettie," Raina said. "The others are human as human can be."

"Well, there is something in that." Nettie downed the rest of her glass. "You get in the dark room. I'll take the rest to get cleaned up before my whole house is covered in bloody footprints."

"How kind of you to worry about our carpet." Raina stood. "You three find me when you've finished washing and sleeping... and dealing with Nettie. If the world hasn't ended by then." With one last glare at Nettie, Raina sauntered out of sight.

"How pleasant," Nettie growled.

"Thank you for your hospitality," Nola said. "Your house is beautiful."

"Thanks." Nettie studied Nola, starting from her toes and moving all the way up. She turned to the decanter and poured herself a fresh drink. "I suppose if I am going to be caught with a fugitive, it might as well be a runaway Domer."

"The men outside," Beauford asked, stepping in between Nola and Nettie, "can they be trusted? If they find out the domes are looking for us, will they tell them to knock on your door?"

"Those men would protect the occupants of Bellevue Avenue with their lives." Nettie waved her drink precariously through the air. "And they have no love for the domes besides. No, the damn Outer Guard will have to track you themselves."

"But won't they know Raina's your sister?" Nola asked. "I mean, if she really is your sister."

"Raina *was* my sister." Nettie smiled ruefully. "A very long time ago. But as for them tracing that colorful-haired Vamper to my home, impossible. The Raina who was my sister is dead."

T stepped forward, reaching out to shake Nettie's hand. "Well then, thank you even more for taking us in."

"Coming from the pregnant girl who I would be a monster to leave on the streets, that means so much." Nettie raised her glass in salute.

"I've been on the street before," T said. "You are being good taking us in, not just avoiding being bad."

"Oh good God, the types my sister drags into this damn house." Nettie rolled her eyes. "Come have a bath and sleep.

Wherever Raina is leading you, I doubt they'll have water as clean as I do, let alone warmed for a bath."

"You have clean water?" Nola asked, moving quickly to match Nettie's stride out of the living room. She hadn't noticed the fine blue wallpaper when they had been in the hall a few moments before, or the big wooden staircase that led to the upper level.

"Not clean by dome standards." Nettie shrugged. "But nothing really is. And aren't impurities what make life worth living?" She took another sip of her drink before heading up the stairs. "I'm going to put you all in one room, and, no offense, I'm locking you in. You seem quite nice, but I have met too many of my sister's compatriots to be able to go back to sleep knowing any of them are wandering the halls."

"We understand," Nola said. "Thank you for letting us stay."

"How gracious of me, I know," Nettie said. "I'll send a touch of food, and the water is drinkable. Try not to get blood on anything."

Nettie swung open the door to a bedroom. T went in first, whistling at the sight of whatever waited inside, Beauford followed after her, but Nola didn't want to let Nettie leave. "You said she's your big sister. Raina, I mean."

Nettie took another drink from her glass. "Yes, little Domer covered in blood, she was my big sister."

T's voice came from within the room. "Can I go first? Do you mind if I go first?"

"But she's, I mean you're—" Nola fumbled for the words.

"Older?" Nettie laughed. "Grayer, smaller, and a bit more sane? Yes, that I am."

"How?" But the answer had already formed in Nola's mind. "Vamp. It's the Vamp. It stops you from aging?"

"They don't tell you anything locked behind the glass, do they? You do age once you've turned to Vamp. Only much more slowly. My sister decided to hide in the darkness a long time ago, and so she's stuck living in the night. A long life without sunrises. It's the blessing and the curse of the damned stuff. And why they can't give it to children. Their bodies need to grow but the Vamp won't let them. So child zombies wander until they rot. Charming, isn't it? A life that won't allow living."

"But if it saves people from dying," Nola said, "doesn't that make it worth it? I mean, not for zombie babies, but for adults. Doesn't the choice come down to vampire or death?"

"For most." Nettie shrugged. "And most definitely for you. But some can skate by living under the ever-killing sun. Forgive me, bloody girl, a few sips of this amazing stuff and I become quite philosophical." She waved Nola toward the open doorway. "Go sleep. I doubt anyone will kill you before it's time to wake up. But for the love of all that survives in this cruel, dark world, please wash your face, child."

She shoved Nola into the room, and a moment later a heavy lock *thunked* behind her.

CHAPTER THIRTY

Nola stood by the locked door, unable to move. The bedroom was different than anything she had ever seen before. It looked like something out of an old novel. A canopy of deep red fabric hung over a four-poster bed, which was wide enough for three people to sleep comfortably in and had a fluffy quilt that perfectly matched the canopy. A fainting couch covered in gold fabric sat at the foot of the bed.

Thick carpeting, so beautiful Nola felt terrible standing on it, covered the floor. And T's voice drifted from the back of the room as she hummed to herself over the sound of running water.

"It's"—Beauford chewed his bottom lip—"something, isn't it?"

"We don't have things like this in the domes." Nola unlaced her boots, leaving them by the door. "I mean, I know we have a lot, but this"—she ran her fingers over the quilt—"this is amazing. I didn't think things like this existed anymore."

"They do." Beauford sat on the fainting couch. "The world didn't end when the domes sealed their walls. At least not entirely. Millions and millions of people have died. More than that have turned to things like Vamp and Lycan to save themselves. But some people profit from death. Some can afford those who call themselves doctors. They'll be the last to go. Or the next. It all depends."

"Depends on what?" she asked, silently sliding the pack off her back and carefully unzipping it.

"Who takes over first." Beauford stared down at his hands. "The domes will let the rich ones out here live because they aren't hurting the domes. They don't need help. They don't want trouble. They are above and below the domes' notice all at once."

Nola pulled the tub of thick blue goo out of her pack.

"But the vampires hate the ones who have managed to survive in comfort on the outside without turning to Vamp. The ones who can afford water purifiers and gardened food. They hate them for proving Vamp isn't the only way to live. So, if the vampires or the wolves manage to take power, Bellevue and the last of the outside luxury are gone."

"But the wolves have already won." She knelt on the couch next to Beauford. His sleeve was fairly intact, but the wound on his arm showed through. "The Outer Guard won't stop them, so why aren't they here?"

She rolled up Beauford's sleeve, expecting with every movement that he would push her away and shout that he didn't need help. But he only watched as she scooped blue goo from the jar and dabbed it onto his arm.

"Because the wolves haven't won. Not really," Beauford said. "The Outer Guard could come across the river and kill them. The vampires in the city could band together and rise up, and worst of all Nightland could return and demand their city back."

"But wouldn't it make sense to take care of Bellevue while they have the chance?" Nola screwed the top of the tub back into place. "Then they can tick one thing off their *to-kill* list."

"Do you want them to come kill us?" Beauford asked.

She shook her head.

"Bellevue is here. It'll always be here. A constant target that would be too risky to take until they know they don't need their muscle in other places. Bellevue doesn't hurt anyone, it just...is. A tiny prickle in the side to remind the poor people others survived." He rolled his sleeve back down, covering the skin Nola had tended to.

"It seems to me that would be more dangerous than anything else. The idea that there can be peaceful life in the light."

"That's the difference between Domers and outsiders." Beauford shook his head, and his shaggy hair covered his eyes. "Domers can argue about thoughts and meaning and ideas. Out here it's about what the food source is and who controls it and who has the medicine you need to get patched up. They'll come for the rich as soon as they have the city. Take the food and the medicine and every last thing they own. They'll fight to the last man just for the joy of seeing them fall."

"I can't—" Nola shut her eyes tight as she zipped her mother's backpack shut. "It's...it's hard for me to believe how much I didn't know. It'll probably get me killed first, right? Like the rich people."

"First." Beauford smiled grimly, his lips pulling into a tight line. "Or last. The domes prepared you to outlive us all, not to actually survive."

"But she can't die first." T stood in the doorway to the bathroom, wrapped in a white towel that made her look younger than ever. "Catlyn already did that. So, you'll just have to die last, Nola." Her words hung in the air for a moment. "The bathroom is all yours, and the soap smells better than flowers."

"Thanks," Nola said. "Just promise you won't be gone when I get out?"

"Don't worry," T said. "We're locked in."

"Right." Nola hesitated for a moment with her hand on the top of her backpack. Raina had the ReVamp. She had the medical supplies and food.

My entire worth is in this backpack.

Nola tightened her fingers on the strap. "I'll be right back."

She lifted the pack and carried it to the bathroom, shutting and locking the door behind her.

She closed her eyes and leaned on the door for a moment, letting the quiet of the room echo in her ears. There was no one trying to capture or kill her in here.

I'm never going to feel safe again.

When she finally managed to open her eyes, she had to blink a few times to be sure she was seeing everything properly.

The floor was bright white marble. A heavy white ceramic sink matched the white ceramic tub. A small chandelier provided the light for the room, its reflection glinting off a mirror that covered half the wall. A girl was reflected in the mirror, too. Logic told Nola it was her, but it didn't seem possible.

She let the backpack slide to the floor, and the girl in the reflection moved just the same way. She stepped closer to the mirror, drawn to the horror she had become.

Her hands and clothes were caked in blood and dirt. Her hair was tangled and filthy, but it was her face she couldn't look away from. Dried blood covered her mouth, a dark red stain that dripped down her throat. She had bitten the man, she had tasted his blood, and the horrible truth of it covered her face. She looked like a vampire. Tears cut wide, pale tracks through the deep red.

She turned on the water as hot as it would go and scrubbed her face in the sink. It didn't matter if the water was contaminated or filthy. She was worse.

She didn't stop scrubbing her face until it was raw, then she climbed into the tub, crouching under the faucet to wash. There was no shower here, and she couldn't bear the thought of soaking in someone else's blood. She should be sobbing. They had left Catlyn in the tunnels. But the tears came slowly as she scraped the blood out from under her nails.

It felt like an eternity before her hands were finally clean. The girl in the mirror looked like her again. Bruised and cut, but her.

She dragged on clean clothes and rinsed the blood out of everything else, without real hope of it being dry when they had to leave. Finally, she grabbed the pack and headed back out to the bedroom.

Beauford and T sat on the bed, a tray of food between them.

"Eat up." T smiled. "There's plenty for all of us."

"Thanks." Nola put the bag in the corner and climbed up onto the giant bed.

"It's good food, too." T handed Nola a piece of bread. "I mean, not dome good, but..." She blushed.

"It's great." Nola took a bite. It was sweeter than dome food, but her stomach growled greedily at the taste of it. "I haven't had much food made outside the domes. We don't have sugar or preservatives in our food. This is nice, just different."

"We won't have anything this good when we get to Nightland," Beauford said. "If we make it there alive."

"Beauford, don't," T said.

"We already lost Catlyn. And we haven't even made it to the city limits," Beauford pushed on.

"Please stop." Tears welled in T's eyes.

"Catlyn was a wonderful woman," he said, the usual gruffness in his voice gone, "but the last thing she would want is for our grieving for her to hurt our chances of survival."

"If you don't want to go to Nightland, then what do you want to do?" T said. "This city is falling. Even if we could stay away from the Outer Guard, how long do you think we would survive?"

"Not long enough for that baby to be born," Beauford said.

T wrapped her arms around her stomach.

"I don't see how this is helping." Nola set her half-eaten slice of bread down on the bed, resisting the urge to wrap an arm around T.

"Catlyn wanted us to get out of the city," Beauford said. "I know that better than anyone. And if we're getting out of the city, the only place any of us knows to go is Nightland."

"Then why are we talking about this?" T asked. "We have to go. If we die, we die, but there's nothing to do but keep trying."

"Because, if I'm hurt as bad as Catlyn, I want ReVamp," Beauford said, looking into both T's and Nola's eyes in turn. "I promised Catlyn I would do whatever it took to get us to Nightland. If that means becoming a Vamper to keep fighting, then I want to do it."

"Okay." T nodded. "I'll make sure you get the injection."

"But you can't take it." A tinge of fear touched Beauford's voice.

"No." T shook her head. "If I die, I die."

Both of them turned to Nola before Beauford asked, "And if you get hurt?"

"What?" Nola pushed herself as far back as the four-poster bed would allow.

"If it comes down to it," he said, reaching across the bed and gripping her hand, "do you want to go like Catlyn, or do you want to be like Raina?"

"I-I," Nola stammered, her mind racing so quickly she could hardly breathe. "That won't happen. We'll be fine. We'll all be fine."

"Catlyn is dead," Beauford said. "I've known Catlyn my whole life. She'd been looking after me since before I could crawl." Pain shot through his voice, and a thick wrinkle appeared between his brows. "I would have given her the shot. I would have made her into a Vamper, saying it was to keep her alive, but really it would've been for my own selfish benefit. Because I didn't want to lose her. I don't know you, *we* don't know you. We're out here with half the city wanting to eat us and the people with fancy guns wanting to catch or kill us, and the one who knows you best is a crazy Vamper with a knife fetish. So, I'm asking you once and for all, Vamper or corpse: what do *you* want?"

She couldn't move. Panic surged through her. Beauford gripped her hand, leaning across their meal, his eyes bright with held-back tears. T was crying in earnest now, wiping her tears away with her still dirty sleeve, which left filth on her cheek.

"I have a clean shirt." Nola wrenched her hand away from Beauford. "You can wear it and wash out yours." She crouched down by her bag, hiding her face from him while she searched for the other shirt.

"We need to know what you want us to do." Beauford jumped off the bed and knelt by her side. "Nola, we need to know."

The use of her name, the sound of it in his voice, stopped Nola's frantic digging.

"We made it this far." He pulled the bag out of her reach. "And that is amazing. But we have a lot farther to go. I know all of us will fight like hell to survive, but I almost went against Catlyn's dying wish because I didn't know any better. I don't want to risk that with anyone else."

"I don't know." Nola's voice came from a million miles away. "I don't know what I want. I want to eat bread and sleep in a bed. I want to find T a clean shirt."

"Leave her alone, Beauford," T said. "She just left her home. Give her a second to breathe."

"Okay." He tossed the bag back to Nola. "But if the time comes, she'll just have to live or die with whatever choice we make for her." Beauford walked into the bathroom, closing the door roughly behind him.

Silence filled the room for a moment. The only sound was Beauford turning on the taps of the bath.

"You have to forgive him," T said. "He's never been great with people, and losing Catlyn is a lot for both of us."

Nola's fingers finally closed around her other clean shirt. "I didn't know you three were so close. I thought you just got grouped together for work in the domes."

"Thanks," T said, taking the shirt Nola offered. "Catlyn was the pied piper of lost children. She had a strong door and a big floor in her apartment, so she would let all of us stay with her when we needed a place out of the rain or away from the riots. I don't know how she scraped it together, but there was always something to eat. Enough to get by until we could find food on our own. She was devastated when I went down to Nightland, thought I would get myself drained by some Vamper. Took her months to even agree to meet Charles, and then when he disappeared, well, she found us work in the domes. And that kept us from starving."

T pulled on Nola's shirt. It was tighter than what T had worn in the domes, hugging her pregnant belly. T's face crumpled as she stared down at her stomach.

"And now Catlyn's gone." T buried her face in her hands. She'd stopped crying. She just looked exhausted.

Hesitantly, Nola stepped forward and wrapped her arms around T.

"I'm so sorry," was all she could think to whisper as T leaned into her shoulder, sagging with the weight of what lay behind and the unknown they had left to face.

CHAPTER THIRTY-ONE

The daylight faded from the crack in the curtain. Nola had been staring at the tiny sliver of light for hours. Every time she fell asleep for a few minutes, a noise would wake her, and she would lay frozen, convinced the Outer Guard had found them.

T lay in the bed next to Nola, her arms wrapped protectively around her stomach.

Beauford was sprawled out on the gold couch at the foot of the bed, breathing slowly and steadily as though fear were a thing he couldn't understand.

Nola pinched her eyes shut, knowing Nettie or Raina would be coming for them soon. They would be back on the streets, walking far at best, fighting for their lives at worst. She needed sleep. Even the few minutes she had left would be valuable. But she couldn't manage it.

Her mother would be in tears. Or furious and refusing to say Nola's name ever again.

Jeremy was probably still out looking for her, convinced she was a brainwashed captive. She wished she could have told them why she had to leave. That the beauty and safety of the domes weren't enough to cover the lies and blood that lay beneath. But then she never would have been able to leave. They would have locked her up in one of the cells.

She rolled onto her back and stared up at the ceiling. She shouldn't feel guilty about Jeremy wasting his time searching for her. He had lied. He had let her be a part of murder. But her mother...

You had to do it. You had to get out. And you saved four people doing it.

Three, a voice whispered in the back of her mind. *You only saved three.*

Finally, a faint rapping sounded on the door followed by the heavy *thunk* of the lock flipping over.

"Wakey, wakey." Raina swung open the door. "My beloved sister wants to offer you one more meal in our house before we run for our lives, so who's hungry?"

"We should all eat," Beauford said, on his feet before either of the girls could climb out of the sheets. "It doesn't matter if we're hungry."

"What about you?" T asked as she pulled on her shoes. "Do you need to eat?"

"How kind of you, worrying about feeding the vampire," Raina said. "Don't worry, I met a tasty little street guard already. I feel fit as a night-walking fiddle."

"Then let's eat and get out of here." Nola picked up her pack. Her back ached in protest.

"I can carry that for you." Beauford reached for the bag.

"No!" Nola said. "I can carry it. I mean, I want to carry it." Her face flushed at Beauford's suddenly stony expression.

"Smart girl," Raina said. "Now eat before it gets completely dark. We can't afford to waste time."

T followed Raina quickly out the door, leaving Nola and Beauford alone.

"I really do appreciate the offer," she said, "but I can carry it myself."

"I wouldn't steal your pack from you." Beauford examined Nola's face. "But I guess you won't believe that, will you? You've been lied to too much. If we live long enough, maybe you'll trust somebody again."

He strode past Nola and out the door, leaving her head spinning. She moved as quickly as she could, grabbing the still-damp clothes she had washed and stuffing them in the top of the pack, making it heavier still, but by the time she reached the downstairs, the others had nearly finished eating.

"Eat up." Nettie raised a crystal glass in welcome. "I made sure the meal was special, a goodbye feast for my sister. Of course, we've had a few of these before, and the goodbye part never does seem to stick."

"Thank you." Nola didn't know what else to say. She slid into the empty seat left at the polished wooden table. A slice of meat and something that looked like potatoes sat on a china plate.

"You know, it's not like I ever *try* to come back here." Raina kicked her feet up, putting her boots on the table. "It just sort of happens, and I do actually own the place, so I think you should be grateful I let you live in my house, baby sister."

Nola shoveled food into her mouth as Nettie's face turned red.

"Your house? Your house! You can't even live aboveground!"

"That's what curtains are for." Raina's eyes sparkled as her sister's anger grew.

"You abandoned this house when you decided to be a Vamper!" Nettie stood, sloshing the pungent liquid from her glass. "Dammit."

"I didn't decide to be a Vamper. I decided to survive," Raina said. "I decided I wanted to survive without all the terribly strict rules that have kept you alive."

"You wanted to run around on the street. You got yourself sick." Nettie pounded her glass down on the table, shattering the crystal. "Shit! You made your choices, and leaving this house forever is your consequence! This is my house." Nettie wrapped a napkin around her bleeding palm.

"I have no intention of taking it from you, little sister." Raina kicked her feet off the table and stood as Nola shoved the last bite of meat into her mouth. "Just remember when I come knocking, you will answer. Or I'll burn the place to the ground and neither of us will have it."

"You are cruel," Nettie said. "You are cruel and psychotic."

"Half of that is reasonably true." Raina waved the others to stand. "But I always have your interests at heart. And your best interest is never to forget you have a vampire sister in Nightland. It might just save you one of these days."

"I don't need your protection," Nettie said.

Beauford took Nola by the elbow and dragged her to the doorway.

T followed, hiding in Beauford's shadow.

"Of course not." Raina walked over to her sister and kissed her on the forehead before Nettie could back away. "Until you do. Try not to die, Nettie. It'd be a pity for the house to be empty."

"How dare—" Nettie began, but Raina had already pushed past Beauford and out into the hall.

"Don't you dare darken my door again!" Nettie shouted after Raina, chasing Nola, Beauford, and T out into the hall. "I won't be taking in anymore of your friends either. I'm done!"

"That's what you said last time." Raina worked swiftly on the seven locks that ran along the side of the door. "And if I do show up again, you'll open the door. Partly because it's my house I let you exist in, but mostly because you love me, baby Nettie, and you'd never leave me out to die in the sun or burn in the rain."

"I will, I swear it!"

"Until next time, sister." Raina flung open the door and stepped into the darkening night.

"Thank you," T whispered as she followed Raina out onto the street.

"Thanks," Beauford mumbled.

"Yes, thank you for your hospitality," Nola echoed and moved to follow.

"Glad to help." Nettie's gaze followed her sister as Raina strode down the road without glancing back. "But you had better follow Raina before she leaves you behind. Who knows how much harder it will be to get yourself killed without her help?"

As soon as Nola was through the door, it slammed behind her. She ran down the street, chasing Raina, the pack bursting pain through her spine as it bounced with every stride.

"Where are we going?" Nola wheezed as soon as she caught up.

"Nightland." Raina led them past the guards who waited in the shadows, winking at one who wore a conspicuous white bandage on his neck.

"I meant more immediately."

"To the western outskirts of the city." Raina turned a corner and led them out of view of Bellevue Avenue. "Then we head out into the wild. There's no point in my telling you where to go after that. You wouldn't find Nightland anyway."

"And if we get separated?" Beauford asked as Raina led them down a street where torches were lashed to the broken lamp-posts. A withered-looking man moved down the road, lighting each post in turn as people began emerging from their houses for the night.

"If we get separated, you're on your own. Find a safe place to wait out the apocalypse and try not to die. I'm not stopping until I get to Nightland."

Nola wanted to think Raina wasn't serious, but she knew her too well.

The city is too dangerous for any of us to risk lingering.

"Hey, you!" a man shouted from the side of the street. His long, matted hair framed his gaunt, gray face. "What are you doing here?"

At the sound of his voice, other people on the street began to take notice of them.

"Passing through," Raina said, not slowing her stride as twelve people closed in around them.

"We don't like Vampers on this street." The man stepped into the light of one of the newly lit torches. The dancing flames glinted off his bright red eyes.

"Didn't know this street had been taken by wolves." Raina spoke as though the fact that they were surrounded by were-wolves was only vaguely interesting.

"Well, it has been, and we don't just let Vampers and humans wander down our street." The man stepped in front of Raina, blocking her path.

"I'm not wandering." Raina's hand tightened around the handle of the metal box she carried. "Actually, I'm in a hurry. So get out of my way."

The man let out a howling laugh that echoed around the street.

"If you don't move, I'll have to hurt you." Raina smiled and stepped so close to the wolf, it looked as though she might kiss him. "It would be a pain in my ass, but I'd win. And then the Outer Guard would come and kill you all. So, move or die."

"The Outer Guard won't come," the man said. "Maybe you don't know they blew up the bridge, just like you don't know werewolves run the city now."

"One." Raina wriggled a finger over her shoulder, beckoning T forward.

"Oh god, she's counting!" A chorus of laughter surrounded them as the wolves came closer.

"Two." Raina pressed the silver box into T's hands.

"Vampers are so cocky," the man sneered. "You really think you can beat a whole street of werewolves?"

"Three." In one, fluid motion Raina grabbed the knife that had been tucked into T's belt and slit the wolf's throat.

Before the man hit the ground, Raina threw T's knife, hitting the wolf that was farthest away right in the eye as she dove toward another, sinking her own knife between his ribs as though he were made of air.

"Anyone else?" Raina asked politely as she pulled her knife from the wolf's chest and raised it to his neck making an incision just the right size for her to eat from. She lowered her mouth and took a long drink, never taking her eyes from the other wolves as she easily supported the dead man that had become her second supper. "No one?" She wiped her mouth on her sleeve. "I forgot how disgusting wolves taste. Someone bring the pregnant girl her knife."

A girl in the back walked to the man who lay face up on the street with a knife sticking out of his eye. Shaking, she grabbed the hilt and pulled. The faint squelching noise made Nola shiver more than the cooling night air had.

Still shaking, the girl ran forward, placing the knife at T's feet before sprinting away.

T picked up the knife and walked over to the first of the wolves Raina had struck, wiping the blood onto his shirt before sliding the blade back into her belt.

"All set?" Raina asked, turning back down the street. "If anyone follows us, I stab them in the heart and make sure they don't get up."

She led them calmly away, not looking back until they rounded the corner and were out of sight. "We need to run, and no one can fall behind."

"What?" Nola turned to look back at where they had left the wolves. "No one's following us."

"I just knifed three wolves in the middle of the street," Raina said. "We're leaving a trail of body-shaped breadcrumbs behind us along with a pack of pissed off wolves. We need to put as much distance between us and them as we can. So we run." She looked at T. "You need me to carry you, baby machine?"

"I'm fine," T said.

"You fall behind, I'm carrying you. You fight me on it, I'll kill you myself," Raina said.

T's nod hollowed out the last of Nola's courage.

"This way." Raina set off down the street.

Keep running.

Nola took a deep breath and followed. She could easily keep pace with T, and Beauford ran in the back as he had done in the woods. She watched Raina's hair streaming behind her, a shimmering flag Nola had to follow if she wanted to get out of the city. She didn't study the buildings where the fronts had crumbled almost entirely away. She didn't stare at the corpse someone had left to bloat in the gutter during the heat of the day. All she could do was follow the blur of scarlet and purple.

The backpack rubbed her back raw, and every time it slammed into her spine, it seemed to steal some of the precious air her lungs were working so hard to use.

"Give me the pack." Beauford's words were uneven as they ran. "It's slowing you down."

"I can do it," Nola panted, her gait faltering as her body begged her to give up the extra weight.

"It's not about what you can do, it's about surviving." He grabbed the loop at the top of the pack, stopping Nola in her tracks. He pulled the bag away from her and had it on his back before she could catch her breath enough to argue.

"Now run," Beauford said.

Side by side they sprinted to catch up to Raina and T.

The sky was fully dark now, and its darkness was easier to see as they made it closer to the outskirts of town. Here there were no torches or streetlamps to light the decaying buildings. The people who were out in this part of the city didn't roam in packs or sit on stoops. The few people they passed either moved nearly as quickly as they did or shambled in the deep shadows.

When Nola's lungs burned so badly it felt like they might

burst, one of the shamblers appeared at the end of a street, moving toward the center of the road as though waiting for them.

Raina pulled her knife and drove it into the person's chest as they ran by. Nola's feet caught the uneven pavement beneath her, and she tumbled forward, catching herself with her hands. Beauford looped an arm around her waist and hoisted her to her feet, not letting go until she was running on her own again.

"She killed him," Nola panted as they ran past the person.

But a brief glance told her that it wasn't a man but a woman. A shriveled woman whose gray hair matched her skin. Angry red splotches and terrible black sores dotted the woman's face. A zombie. Raina had been right to kill the poor woman.

"T!" Beauford's shout pulled Nola's attention back to the road ahead of them. T limped, favoring one ankle as she tried to keep up with Raina.

"I'm fine," T panted.

Raina turned and raced back to T, scooped her into her arms, and was running again without breaking her stride.

They had to be near the end. Surely, the edge of the city would come soon.

Inside her shoes, Nola could feel the skin on her feet tearing. Her legs felt like lead, spots danced before her eyes, but she had to keep running.

"Halt!" the shout cut through the night.

Nola faltered for a moment, just long enough for Beauford to smack into her. She pitched forward again, but Beauford grabbed her, dragging her into the shelter of a stoop as a string of tiny *pops* pierced the night.

CHAPTER THIRTY-TWO

"Magnolia Kent, are you hurt?" a voice shouted.

"The Outer Guard found us," Nola whispered, sure Beauford knew what was happening but needing to say the words aloud so she could feel them in her mouth. They had only been out of the domes for a day, and the Outer Guard had already found them.

"Magnolia Kent," the voice shouted again. "Are you hurt?"

"She's fine," Raina shouted, "but you won't be if you don't get out of our way."

"Magnolia Kent," the voice shouted again. "Are you hurt?"

"I'm fine." Tears stung Nola's eyes. "None of these people hurt me. They would never hurt me."

"Magnolia, come down to the end of the street slowly."

"Promise you won't hurt them!" Nola shouted. "Promise you'll let them leave, and I'll come with you."

"Nola, no." Beauford grabbed her wrist. "Going with them won't make things any better for us."

"But it might buy you some time." Nola leaned around the edge of the steps. "Promise me you won't hurt them, and I'll do whatever you want."

"Fine," the guard called quickly. Much too quickly for an order to have been decided upon.

"Run," Nola said. "I'll try to keep them busy. Get as far away from here as you can."

"We can't just leave you with them."

"You can and will. The Guard's guns can do worse than sedate people. Get to T and get out." Nola stood and walked out to the center of the street. Beauford had the pack. She was glad he had taken it. Maybe it would help the others survive on their way to Nightland.

Moving as slowly as she dared, Nola headed toward the end of the road. Two men in Outer Guard uniform faced her, guns raised.

"Two?" Nola coughed a laugh. "They only sent two guards to take me back?"

"There are Outer Guard all over the city, Magnolia. We're just the ones that found you." The guard's face was hidden behind his helmet's visor, but Nola imagined him smiling. Captain Ridgeway would be so proud of the guards who captured the runaways.

"Two alone won't be able to stop the ones I've got with me." Nola paused in the middle of the street. "You should have followed us quietly, waited for others to come."

"We have guns," the other guard said. "They have none."

"She doesn't need a gun."

No sooner had the words left Nola's lips than a whizzing sound came from the shadows, and two knives sank into the throats of the guards. Both men gasped and gurgled as they fell to the ground.

"Found a way around the coat problem." Raina stepped out of the shadows. "I mean, coats that block weapons, what fun is—"

A howling scream from the end of the street cut off Raina's words.

"You think you can murder us and get away with it?"

A group of thirty wolves rounded the corner, the girl who had given T back her knife at the front of the pack.

"You think you can walk down our street and we'll let you disappear? Shouting to tell us where you were, that was so helpful. Naïve, and deadly, but terribly helpful."

"I'm surprised it took you so long to catch up." Raina smiled, backing away from the wolves toward the downed guards.

"No, you don't get your knives back," the girl growled, crouching in a frighteningly animalistic way before leaping forward with a howl.

Beauford grabbed Nola's arm, pulling her forward as the wolves charged. Raina ran ahead of them. She would reach the knives before the wolves could reach her, but the pack was right on Nola's heels.

"No!" T screamed.

Nola glanced over to see three big male wolves backing T into a corner.

"Please!" T begged. "Please, I'm pregnant."

Nola heard the wolves laugh as something heavy collided with her spine, knocking her to the ground. But the heavy thing was pulled away as Beauford bellowed, "Leave her alone!"

As Nola scrambled to her feet, Beauford punched the wolf in the face, but there were more of them coming.

Nola ran as fast as she could, all thoughts of fear gone. Most of the pack had gone straight for Raina, who fought the snarling mass, a knife in each hand.

Nola ran past the wolves to the two bleeding Outer Guard. Each of them still held a gun in their limp hands. Her fingers trembled as she grabbed them both.

Her father had let her hold his gun years ago, taken her down to the training room to fire it.

The safety was off.

She pulled the trigger, trusting the clip of tiny silver needles would still be loaded.

Pop.

A needle shot from the gun, missing the nearest wolf by a foot.

Pop, pop, pop.

The wolf who had knocked the knife from Raina's left hand fell.

Pop, pop.

Another wolf fell.

She aimed farther away to the wolf that had Beauford pinned to the ground.

Pop, pop, pop, pop, pop.

A silver needle sank into the man's shoulder, and he fell on top of Beauford, who pushed the man off him and ran toward T.

Nola aimed for the wolves that had surrounded T.

Pop, pop, pop, pop.

Needles sank into two of the wolves, but Beauford had closed in. She couldn't risk hitting him.

She looked back at Raina.

Pop.

One of the wolves looked behind as the man fighting next to him fell. His eyes locked on Nola, and he charged.

Nola raised the gun to shoot again.

Click.

The first gun was empty, but before Nola could lift the other, the wolf leapt, striking her in the chest and knocking her to the ground. Her head cracked on the pavement, and stars swam in front of her eyes.

"You stupid little girl." The man pressed on her wrists and dug his knee into her chest. She still clutched the loaded gun, but she couldn't move her hand to aim it.

He let go of her arm and raised a knife high in the air. Nola aimed and pulled the trigger. A silver needle disappeared into the man's neck a moment too late.

The filthy blade sank into Nola's stomach. Pain like fire soared through her as a scream tore from her throat.

The man toppled sideways, wrenching the knife from her flesh as he fell. Nola screamed again as the pain doubled. Her shaking fingers found the warm blood that seeped from her stomach.

"Help," Nola croaked. "Help."

But Raina was still fighting three of the wolves, blood coating her back.

I hope she survives. I hope the three of them survive.

"No. No!"

Someone was screaming from down the street, farther away than Nola could see.

"Nola!"

The stars above shimmered in and out of being. Blackness pulsed at the edges of Nola's mind.

"Raina!" Beauford's voice shouted.

There was a scream of pain, and then another.

I hope that's not me screaming.

"Nola." Beauford's face swam into view as he pressed hard on the part of her stomach torn by the knife. The pain tripled.

She wanted to tell him to stop, there was too much damage to press it away, but the pain had made it impossible to form words.

"Nola," Beauford shouted. "Stay with me, Nola."

"You're okay." T was there, her face bruised, but she was alive and breathing. "You're going to be okay."

Nola smiled.

There was more shouting, more fighting. They needed to run.

"Nola!" Beauford shouted again.

It took Nola's eyes a moment to focus on his face. He looked frightened and pale in the moonlight.

"Nola, we need to know," he spoke slowly as though determined for her to understand. "Nola, ReVamp or death? We need to know what you want us to do. Do you want the shot? Nola, Nola!"

The sound of her name being shouted followed her into darkness.

"Nola!"

The Girl of Glass series continues with *Night of Never*.

Thank you for reading *Boy of Blood*. If you enjoyed the book, please consider leaving a review to help other readers discover the series.

As always, thanks for reading,

Megan O'Russell

Never miss a moment of the danger or romance.

Join the Megan O'Russell mailing list to stay up to date on all the action by visiting https://www.meganorussell.com/book-signup.

ABOUT THE AUTHOR

Megan O'Russell is the author of several Young Adult series that invite readers to escape into worlds of adventure. From *Girl of Glass*, which blends dystopian darkness with the heart-pounding danger of vampires, to *Ena of Ilbrea*, which draws readers into an epic world of magic and assassins.

With the *Girl of Glass* series, *The Tethering* series, *The Chronicles of Maggie Trent*, *The Tale of Bryant Adams,* the *Ena of Ilbrea* series, and several more projects planned, there are always exciting new books on the horizon. To be the first to hear about new releases, free short stories, and giveaways, sign up for Megan's newsletter by visiting the following:

https://www.meganorussell.com/book-signup.

Originally from Upstate New York, Megan is a professional musical theatre performer whose work has taken her across North America. Her chronic wanderlust has led her from Alaska to Thailand and many places in between. Wanting to travel has fostered Megan's love of books that allow her to visit countless new worlds from her favorite reading nook. Megan is also a lyricist and playwright. Information on her theatrical works can be found at RussellCompositions.com.

She would be thrilled to chat with you on Facebook or Twitter

@MeganORussell, elated if you'd visit her website MeganORussell.com, and over the moon if you'd like the pictures of her adventures on Instagram @ORussellMegan.

ALSO BY MEGAN O'RUSSELL

The Girl of Glass Series

Girl of Glass

Boy of Blood

Night of Never

Son of Sun

The Tale of Bryant Adams

How I Magically Messed Up My Life in Four Freakin' Days

Seven Things Not to Do When Everyone's Trying to Kill You

Three Simple Steps to Wizarding Domination

Five Spellbinding Laws of International Larceny

The Tethering Series

The Tethering

The Siren's Realm

The Dragon Unbound

The Blood Heir

The Chronicles of Maggie Trent

The Girl Without Magic

The Girl Locked with Gold

The Girl Cloaked in Shadow

Ena of Ilbrea

Wrath and Wing

Ember and Stone

Mountain and Ash

Ice and Sky

Feather and Flame

<u>Guilds of Ilbrea</u>

Inker and Crown

Myth and Storm

<u>Heart of Smoke</u>

Heart of Smoke

Soul of Glass

Eye of Stone

Ash of Ages